COPYWRITER

COPYWRITER

A Life of Making Ads and Other Mistakes

Ray Welch

Permissions, Hot House Press
760 Cushing Highway
Cohasset, MA 02025

Library of Congress Control Number: 2001099330
ISBN 0–9700476–4–9
Printed in the United States of America

Book design by DeNee Reiton Skipper

Hot House Press
760 Cushing Highway
Cohasset, MA 02025
www.hothousepress.com

To Gail

Contents

Foreword

When I got my start in 1975—running the stat machine and pasting up at Hill, Holliday, Connors, Cosmopulos—Ray Welch was already top of mind as one of the most colorful characters in the business.

He'd worn a path to the Hatch and Art Directors Club stages. Both his professional accomplishment and high jinks were regularly chronicled in the ad rags and spoken of over see-throughs at Joseph's. He wrote beautifully. It was well known that all his creative was first rate, he played hard, and could laugh harder.

When I finally got to know Ray, I realized immediately that storytelling was actually his great gift. And that his writing was just like his storytelling. Now, whenever I read an ad that Ray has written, I can hear his voice—yep, *that* voice—clear as a martini, up. I've come to appreciate that Ray's work has an abiding, unselfconscious honesty, because it is so unmistakably him.

A few months ago, Ray asked if I would consider designing a chapter in *Copywriter,* a collection of his stories. He'd already signed up the best local art directors of our generation, and he'd finally worked his way down to me, but I was thrilled to be asked and agreed immediately.

As it worked out, we pre-published "The Killington Pitch" as an eBook on partnersandsimons.com—complete with audio—to generate interest in *Copywriter,* and to add some much-needed class to our Internet presence.

Ongoing thanks to Nancy Carle for her help designing the eBook, to Anthony Henriques for his collaboration on "The Portuguese Club," and to Ray, of course, for letting us shamelessly hitch the PARTNERS+simons wagon to his Saab.

Copywriter is full of great stories, told in that sonorous, smoky voice of his. It's a beautifully written chronicle of the ad wars, the way they were in the times of magic markers, hand-rendered layouts, black illustration board, wing-and-a-prayer pitches, and typewriters that went *"ding."*

Tom Simons

Prologue

L ast year I wrote the thing. In a minute, I'll tell you why. To a copy-writer, a "minute" means about 175 words, spoken without rush-ing—the length of a one-minute radio commercial.

It was a pile of work, but I write ads for a living, and I figured 40,000 words was sort of like writing a four-hour radio spot.

Then I figured, Hey, these are stories about advertising (well, loosely) so why not invoke the disciplines of the craft. In which copy and art collaborate to take a message to a new level. Call up twenty of my favorite art directors and designers[1] and ask them to pitch in, shape a chapter or two through their unique jaundiced eyes.

Don't ever do that. It squares and cubes the hassle factor, cost, angst, and vomiting on the part of the writer and publisher. It's like inviting twenty sociopaths to your tea party and handing them each a bottle.

Art directors create problems where none exists—just to put as much pressure as possible on everyone else connected with the project. They hallucinate Killer Flaws that must be sniffed out, hunted down, and fetched to you gently in their mouths.

In creating *Copywriter,* it was deadlines.

---

[1]At first, I even invited other copywriters to climb aboard. Of the twenty people I asked, everyone thought this sort of "oral history" of the industry, during one of its most interesting times, was a hell of an idea. I suspect most of them still do. But only my friend Bill Heater actually sent me something, and my com-puter ate it. So much for that idea.

For sure, I used to deal with deadline problems—real ones—when I was a full-time, working creative director. But back then I could do more to solve them than just threaten to hold my breath until I turned dead.

In fact, I got pretty deft at it.

For example, Karen would come to my office and tell me she couldn't meet a Monday deadline.

"Sorry about that. You're fired," I would console.

"But today is Thursday and I have to have two wisdom teeth pulled tomorrow."

"I understand. About the teeth. You're fired."

"And my boyfriend is flying in from Tokyo just to see me for a few hours this weekend."

"Good for him, Karen. Shows he cares. You're fired."

From my experience—and I was quick to point this out—doing layouts while bleeding from the mouth and sharing intense moments never used to get in the way of making good ads.

But this nifty trick doesn't work so well when you're calling up asking for freebees.

The art directors you'll meet here are as different as hogs and pigs.

Some of them, like Tyler Smith, are the essence of elegance and restraint. If Earth were about to be blasted to bits by a comet tomorrow, and Smitty were designing the front page of *The National Inquirer,* the banner headline would probably read:

World Ends Tomorrow

In a tasteful 8-point GillSans, with italics to underscore the hot news. To make it look more important than:

Yankees Beat Sox

Others, like Dick Pantano, are as in-your-face as they were in the sixties. (Pantano designed "Question #1," which could have been one of his call-to-riot political brochures from the time.)

It is easy—and commonplace—to curdle the friendliness of an ad. I've written hundreds of them that never got read because of lousy art direction: The typeface was hostile (6-point Helvetica reversed out of black springs to mind), the use of color was arbitrary, the photography sucked, the design was banal, the warmth was that of a foreclosure notice.

The art directors and designers you'll see here invite you into the house. You can smell the coffee.

What's the difference between an art director and a designer? A copywriter would tell you this:

Art directors have brains. Designers have eyes. Seldom does either have both.[2]

The great ones do. They're smart enough to help come up with a good idea, and they're visual enough to know how to present it. They know if an ad should shout or whisper. If it should speak in serif or sans serif. If it needs color or can make do with black-and-white. If it needs illustration, or just a readable typeface that doesn't get in the way.

Despite this rambling preamble, I consider myself a minimalist. If you don't need it, don't say it. And I like working with art directors of kindred ilk. If the headline says TRUCK, for God's sake don't show me a layout that features some big honking truck[3]. If the copy talks in a single tone of voice, don't read it to me in different typefaces. And don't mess around with a classic face by adding some faddy kerning or leading.

I once asked one of our art directors what he thought of Mike, a designer we were thinking of hiring. "I don't like his work," he said. "He spreads his type."

These days, one of the most common things to screw up the look of ads is the computer. With a click, you can choose from hundreds of different typefaces. The horror is that many art directors choose to use all of them—in the same ad. The result is visual chaos.

There is seldom a decent reason to use more than two different fonts in an ad—one for the headline, maybe another for the body copy, and then…lower your voice.

----

[2] Another difference is that while most art directors can't draw, most designers can't draw even worse.
[3] In the mid-sixties, Volkswagen did a wonderful ad whose headline was "Truck." The picture was of a VW bus.

For that matter, most designers might be well served to go into their Macs and trash all but half-a-dozen fonts. Throw away Uncle Bill, Clown, Olde English, Impact, Script, and all the other graphical gadgets that might have been okay in a RUNAWAY SLAVE! notice.

Over the years, I've asked some of my favorite art directors and typographers which ten fonts they'd rescue if all the others were drowning in a boat together. Opinions differed—but not by much. Almost everyone's list contained the following families of faces:

Century
Franklin Gothic
Futura
Garamond
Goudy
Helvetica
Palatino

But we're getting into trivia here. This book isn't about making ads look good or sound good. It's not even about making ads. It's about what happens when you crash the gates of the Industry, find a desk somewhere, engage with your creative counterparts, convince a client to pay good money for what his cousin Sylvia would have given him for free, run your own shop, survive in the village (yes, the industry felt more like a home town than most home towns ever do), and apply the stuff you learned in the process to life outside of hucking cars and stereos.

It's also about things that just sort of happen along the way. Like finding my genetic mother ("Ruth") and how to choose the Unique Selling Proposition when you're firing a gun while running naked in the street ("The Hat").

I tend to write in straight lines, disregard didactical syntactical conventions, and get to the point as fast as I can. Even if that means using sentence fragments and one-word paragraphs.

So it always pleases me when an art director takes my plain words and adds a dimension that amplifies their impact and sturdies up their meaning.

I hope you notice and enjoy this dimension, these different treatments of what began as naked pages of words.

M ost of the people I invited to this party are friends I've worked with over the years, and with whom I've shared the irritating, inebriating process of getting an ad from the idea stage to the printed page.

Same with the photographers and illustrators who donated their work.

They range from well-known artists like Ken Maryanski, to unknown-for-a-reason Dan ("Shaky") Reeves, whose line drawing of an ashtray defiles the end of this Introduction.

The photographers go from megabucks-per-day John Goodman, who shot the lousy picture of me and Ali in "The Voter Education Project" to Susan Rankin who shot the stuff for "Cronies," whose price was a pint at Aidan's.

Some of the photos, I plain forget who took them, and I regret not crediting the artists. Especially the shots of Boston Mayor Kevin White in "Question #1." Art director Dick Pantano can't remember either. Please don't sue me for unlicensed use.

The one to sue is Pantano.

"Two Ice Cubes Making Out" by Dan Reeves.

S OME PEOPLE CALL THEM HOVEES. As in Jehovah's Witnesses. But no matter what denomination they are, you can spot them from a block away. Giving you time to shut off the lights and pretend you're not home.

But the window in my study faces the wrong direction to see people a block away, so I answered the door chime.

Two Hovees, standing on my doorstep in the starting snow. One, a clean-cut young man in a dark suit and tie. The other, an octogenarian woman in a black frock and a black hat with fake flowers in it. She carried a vinyl briefcase stuffed with brochures, and swayed a lot.

"Please come in," I said.

They stood in the foyer.

"We'll take only a moment of your time, sir. But I'm sure, like most of us, that you're concerned about the morality of our times. The crisis now before us in government."

As she spoke, the 2000 Presidency was being coin-flipped in Florida. As of ten o'clock this December morning there were still no tanks rumbling down Pennsylvania Avenue.

She went on. "And I'm sure you're sorely troubled by the hanky-panky in the White House. So I've brought some literature you'll find enlightening."

"Forgive me, ma'am, but I don't want any literature."

"But surely, sir, as a man of age, you'd like to see a return to morality?"

The phrase hit me. "A man of age." With the same sly lilt as "A person of color."

Like I'd grown a new skin. The old one having been shed. So my answer might be different from what it might have been before molting season. Maybe I'd slid into the last scene of the four-act play that reprises a copywriter's career:

"Who's Ray Welch?"

"Get me Ray Welch."

"Get me a young Ray Welch."

"Who's Ray Welch?"

I'd never considered myself an Old Man before. I'm 61, on my back nine but not exactly infirm or drooling. But here's this elder in a black hat hanging a label around my neck.

Which is why "man of age" intrigues me.

I'm sure the woman was trying to be kind. But she was telling me, in code, that what she saw was a *geezer*. Because she was well brought up she wouldn't say, "As a geezer, sir..." So she cranked the diction down a notch to, "As a man of age, sir..." But I knew what she meant. Just as a "person of color" knows. You're one of them. Or one of us.

So wasn't I fearful, she asked, brandishing her briefcase, about the Morality of our Times?

I thought for a minute.

I thought about the comforting signs I saw years ago in civic centers, assuring us white folks that this was our own private bubbler or bathroom. About the waves of awareness that crashed as loud as bombs in Vietnam onto campuses and Congressmen. About my wife Gail and all the other smart, good women who could find no job that didn't have a typewriter, telephone or steno pad as part of the package. And get me some coffee, please.

"No," I said to the Hovee lady. "I think we've come a long way in the last few decades. We're going through glitches. Glitches happen. We get past them."

They went away, bearing their briefcases to other doors.

I don't know why, but as I watched the two of them trudge away through the snow to alert my neighbors about moral decay and hanky-panky in the White House, I thought of what one of my kids said to me last Christmas when I went on a storytelling rant, stories about the advertising industry, and how they go toward answering the final-act question, "Who's Ray Welch?"

She said, "Hey, Dad, before you die you ought to write down some of this stuff." (Gail has to remind me from time to time that we all have the same death rate. That being 100% or so.)

Maybe that's why the woman's words stuck with me. "A man of age." And I said to myself, "For God's sake Ray, write it down, you old fool."

Art Direction / Tyler Smith
Production / Terry Morris

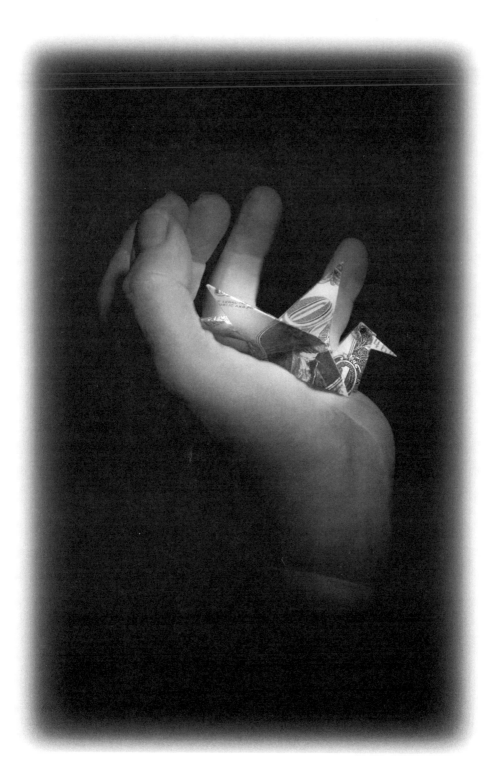

The Bidding War

i n the fall of 1961, after four years at Dartmouth College, I found that I was qualified, barely, to drive a delivery truck around Boston for $47.50 a week—this to support an apartment ($87.50/mo.), a beer habit ($15/mo.), and a wife (whatever was left).

In the glove compartment of my truck I kept a balled-up greenish suit and a fresh *Boston Globe*, the classifieds of which I read every day on coffee break, looking for either a writing job at any price, or $100 a week at any other job in the world.

One day there were two ads for copywriters. One at a place with lots of initials, the other at Atlas Advertising. A solid-sounding place. Logo of a man carrying the world on one shoulder.

I called them first, and got an appointment for four o'clock with their president, Arthur Green. The other place, BBD&O, said be there at two and ask for Marty Conroy. Which I did.

Conroy was short, bald and tough-looking. He smoked cigarettes and drank Pepsi. He read through some of the stuff I'd written for the *Jack-O-Lantern*, Dartmouth's humor magazine. He said, "I've seen worse, I've seen better."

I felt like telling him "Oh yeah? Did you catch the symbolism?" Thinking that would be useful in the ad biz.

"You'll work there," he said, pointing to a small room with no door. "You'll make $60 a week. After a month you get to take your jacket off."

My first job offer as a Writer.

"Thank you, Mr. Conway."

"Conroy."

"Let me give you a call, let you know. Tomorrow morning first thing."

"Tomorrow? What tomorrow?"

"I have another interview this afternoon, and it would only be fair."

"Where's your interview? Who with?"

"Atlas."

"Who?"

"Atlas Advertising. They're in Brookline," I said, explaining everything. Brookline is the next town west of Boston. It is not real famous for its advertising industry.

Marty looked at me like he hadn't noticed my other head at first.

"Sure. Why don't you give me a call, then." And that was the end of the interview. I picked up my writing samples and put them back in their brown paper *Stop & Shop* bag, went back to my truck, and drove to Atlas.

Arthur R. Green (I learned later that behind his back his employees called him "ARG!") was a thin handsome man with dark hair, a good suit, a certificate on his wall saying he had attended a night course at Harvard, and another one attesting to his membership in the Young Presidents Club.

"I see you went to Dartmouth, Mr. Welch." On his desk I'd fanned six copies of the *Jack-O-Lantern*. Stories replete with symbolism. None of which he opened. "There is something to be said for the Ivy League."

I didn't mention that I'd flunked my comps and never got around to graduating, but then he never asked me. Come to think of it, nobody has ever asked me if I graduated, let alone can I have a look at your diploma. Might as well have said I went to Oxford, on full scholarship, athletic as well as academic. "Rowing, you know. Plus Sanskrit Studies. Bloody shame we gave up India."

"Can you start on Monday, Mr. Welch?"

"Could I ask how much you're paying, Mr. Green?"

"Sixty dollars a week." Same as BBD&O.

I told him I had just been offered that very amount, this very afternoon. Letting him know he'd better do better.

He did. "We'll go seventy."

"Let me call you first thing."

But first I called Marty Conroy.

"Mr. Conway? Atlas offered me seventy."

"Who the fuck is Atlas? Again?"

"I think they're an advertising agency."

As it turned out, they weren't. They did syndicated bank ads and state-ment-stuffers, and made their money mostly on the printing. "See this handsome full-color brochure, Harry? *Your* bank could send such a piece to all your customers. For only pennies per. That's because we print up millions at a time. With an imprint area. This space here, we print Your Bank Name."

Mr. Green gave me a few samples of Atlas's product as I was leaving. One piece was a statement-stuffer promoting car loans. On the cover it showed a car key. The headline was "Swing into Spring with a Low-Cost Auto Loan from BANK NAME HERE!" Another stuffer adver-tised mortgages. The cover showed a house key. The headline said "Your Key to Home Ownership! A Low-Cost Mortgage with BANK NAME HERE!"

And Marty Conroy had never heard of Atlas.

But he said, "Christ on a crutch, we'll give you eighty. See you Monday morning first thing."

So I called Mr. Green back. Not knowing, not having a clue, that this was not how you played the game. And told him of the staggering offer from BBD&O.

Long pause. "We can go as high as ninety," he said.

Let me tell you an Arthur Green story that happened years later. It's said that he was negotiating with a Creative Director from New York. Over dinner, Arthur decided he wanted the guy, and popped the ques-tion: "Tell me, Mr. Smith, would you come here for forty thousand?"

"Yes."

Long pause. Like the one he used on me. "Then tell me," he paused even longer. "Would you come here for *thirty?*"

It wasn't until later in life that I learned you didn't dick around with weekly salaries, when the round numbers of annuals covered a lot of short-money pay raises. Or even better, the way I do it now, by the project. Because nobody bothers to do the day-rate math on the fly. But back then, all I knew was I'd just been offered twice what I was making per week driving the delivery truck. Which may still have my greenish suit in its glove compartment.

But I was still moving and shaking.

"Mr. Connelly? Atlas offered me ninety," I said, getting good with this money talk.

I can only picture Marty Conroy staring at the receiver. Opening a Pepsi, lighting a cigarette, sliding out of his sport coat, maybe motioning a few cronies over to listen in on the speaker phone.

"Ah, Ray," he sighed. "Ninety, that's a pile of money. You know, I'd probably have to get an okay from New York to go any better than that. You hear what I'm saying?"

I guess what I heard then was that BBD&O was a Boston branch of an even bigger office in New York. What I heard later was they had offices in London and Chicago and the West Coast and Sydney and where in the world would you like to live, Ray? And that they were the hottest shop, in terms of creative, ever to grace the advertising skyline of New England. Since then, many good agencies have come and gone in Boston, my own among them. But never had any shop so dominated the region as did BBD&O in the 1960s.

A fact I was to learn two months later at my desk at Atlas. Where I'm thinking, "Man, if this is advertising then maybe I should try journalism." There were just so many different keys you could put on the cover of a statement-stuffer.

My Art Director pal was a good-hearted man named John Francis, who kept a large leather-like briefcase hidden behind his flat file. One day, as he was replacing it there, casting guilty glances over his shoulder, I asked him, "So John, what's with the case?"

He glanced around and lowered his voice. ARG! had ears everywhere. "That's my book."

"Your book? You writing a book?"

"No, my portfolio."

"What's a portfolio?"

"That's where you put your samples, your best stuff. And you read the Help Wanteds, and take your book into Boston and try and get a job at a shop like BBD&O."

In December, Marty Conroy called me at the office. To let me know that BBD&O had just announced their Christmas bonus. This year it was going to be two months' salary, and sorry he couldn't have beaten the $90 a week I was getting at Atlas. Tell you the truth, I didn't notice any sarcasm. Marty was good that way.

Three years later he called me again. This time from BBD&O/New York, where he was Creative Director on the Pepsi account and some other major business, and he wanted me to fly down and talk about a job, which I did. But by now I was a CD myself, at Ingalls, with a staff of copywriters who loved me and couldn't possibly survive without me. "You know how it is, Marty."

I'm sure he did. And, on reflection, probably still knows me as one of the biggest jerks ever to bedevil his life.

Art Direction / Jim Richard
Design / Kristen Yanvary
Photography / Christian Delbert

Busy Bakers Bank At Shawmut

Bill Ganick charged into my office carrying a layout pad. "I want you to help out on the Shawmut account."

"What do you need, Mr. Ganick?"

"Cartoons," he said.

"I'm a writer. I'm no good at cartoons."

"You don't have to draw the damn things. Just come up with the situation and write the caption."

Ganick was a Creative Director at Harold Cabot & Son Advertising in 1962. I'd been there for two weeks, after my debacle at Atlas Advertising, and still didn't know a damn thing about the craft. Harold Cabot, Jr. was my boss, the copy chief, and neither did he.

So this was my big chance, my first chance, to work with an old pro, a creative cornerstone of Cabot, the biggest and oldest WASP agency in Boston and, in retrospect now, one of the least creative shops in the country. But they had a lock on all the big utilities in the area: Boston Gas, New England Telephone, New England Electric Systems, and if I remember right, a coal company.

Reading (pronounced "redding") Anthracite. Believe it or not, a branded coal.

Can you imagine calling your local oil company and saying, "Hey, can you send over 100 gallons of Atlantic Richfield fuel oil? The tank's running low." No. You would say, "Hey, can you deliver us some oil before the damn pipes freeze?"

But not Reading Anthracite. They wanted people to ask for their coal by name, demand nothing less. "And don't you guys show up here with no damn generic coal, hear?"

So Cabot wrote them a jingle. It went like this:

"When you see coal with red spots bright,

That's famous Reading Anthracite." (Ding!)

"Red spots bright?" Yes.

If you guessed for ten years why "red spots
bright" appears in the Reading Anthracite jingle,
you would never crack it, so I will tell you.

Reading Anthracite,
world's first
"branded" coal.
Imagine the white
dots are "red spots
bright."

They painted the coal. That's right, they spray-painted the
coal lumps with little red dots.

Branding, back in the '60s. Long before Nike.
The "swoosh" of coal.

Red spots bright.

My job was to help brand Shawmut, a bank with
New England's most-recognized Seen/Associated
logo: the sculpted visage of a pissed-off Indian.

The Indian stared at you from billboards, print
ads, television commercials, bank signage,
statement stuffers, you name it. He stared from
everywhere. And he stared at you hard. Just what you
wanted in a banker.

He would be the signature on the ads I was going to write. The
solemn stone face in the lower right-hand corner of the
cartoons under which would be my captions. My captions.

Like "Busy Bakers Bank at Shawmut."

This is what Mr. Ganick explained as he waved his
felt-tip marker at his layout pad, tore off the top
page and slapped it face-down on my desk. "We could
show a baker trying to do two or three things at
once."

"Like what?"

"Like sliding shit in and out of an oven."

I was starting to get it.

"Here's another one," he said, waving the marker. "Friendly Farmers Bank at Shawmut. And we'll show a farmer. Smiling."

He tore off the page and slammed it onto my desktop. "Harried Husbands Bank at Shawmut," he said, "but that one isn't quite there yet. You can tweak it."

"When do you need it?"

"Let's see something by 3:30." He shoved the layout pad pages toward me and strode out of my office. It was now about 4:45. And in those days, if ever, I don't think Bill Ganick drank.

I lit a cigarette. Then I slid the three pages in front of me, one by one, and carefully turned them over.

They were blank.

I figured I'd just had my first brush with greatness.

Art Direction and Illustrations / Rich Kirstein

"Goy, Vey."

A Jewish Agency

The reason I went to Ingalls Advertising was the Volkswagen account.

Outside of Doyle Dane Bernbach, only one agency in the country had a piece of the VW business, and that was Ingalls. The reason I went there. From Cabot, a respected WASP agency handling the profitable, if not prestigious, utilities industries, to a little-known Jewish agency handling accounts like Moxie, a dying soft drink brand (which may still be writhing somewhere).

Yes, advertising agencies then were actually classified, mostly without malice, as WASP and Jewish.[1] With a name like Harold Cabot & Son, that was a WASP agency for sure. And Maslow Gold & Rothschild wasn't.

Neither was Marvin & Leonard, the first names of two guys whose last names were Phyte and Kanzer. Don't ask me why they used their first names instead of their last. (Although Sally Jackson, a public relations person who once worked at Marvin & Leonard, said it was because they thought Phyte Kanzer sounded too much like a slogan for the United Way.)

Schlepper

The founder of Ingalls Advertising, even though Ingalls could sound Jewish, was actually an old-money Yankee who collected rugs and did the *New York Times* crossword every day in his office the size of a conference room, which it ultimately became. After Joe Maynard and Joe Hoffman bought out Arthur Ingalls, they ran the agency from the same desk, literally side by side behind what looked like a door set parallel to the floor on top of two filing cabinets. Maybe it was.

Joe Maynard was the only other non-Jew at Ingalls except for George Smith, an account guy who always struck me as anti-Semitic. If you could label jokes that started with "There was a Catholic, a Protestant and a Hebe who go into a bar . . ." as anti-Semitic. Anyway, in a company of thirteen people, I was only the third goy. So there was always enough for a minion.

Nor had I ever heard a word of Yiddish, except maybe for "schmuck." So when one of my co-workers said, "Welch, as a copywriter you're a real schlimazel," I took it as a compliment.

Until Harold Turin and Avner Rakov took me to lunch, told me they loved me and, for my self-preservation, gave me two books: *The Joys of Yiddish* and *A Treasury of Jewish Quotations*, by Leo Rosten, a scholar who loves the language even more than I do. I still own and read them.

Schmuck

Just as the Eskimos are said to have dozens of different words for "snow," Yiddish has dozens of words describing defects in human intelligence or character. All with varying shades of meaning. Like "powder" is different from "corn snow." But in Yiddish a whole lot of them start with the "sh" sound.

As in schmuck, schlimazel, schlepper, schnook, shnorrer, schlemiel, schmendrik, schmaltz . . . What wonderful words to paint with. Each a different, distinctive, pejorative shade of gray.

On the golf course I still say things like, "I think I hooked it into the schmetz." Even if you don't know what it means, you know what it means.

A guy was putting once, a stranger, wearing a chai around his neck, part of a threesome I got hooked up with on a public course, and he nailed a downhill thirty-footer that must have had a ten-foot break. Fabulous putt. "A mitzvah," I told him. Mitzvah meaning a good deed. As if "from God."

"What does someone named Welch know from mitzvahs?" he said.

I wanted to tell him, "The early days at Ingalls. A Jewish agency."

Schmaltz

Art Direction / Penny Schuler & Keith Lane

[1]Despite the goyified name, Keith Lane is a wear-it-on-your-sleeve Jew, who donates a lot of his time—and sense of humor—to Jewish charities and organizations. A few years ago he was asked to design a poster for the Maccabbee Youth Games, an international athletic competition for Jewish teenagers. He used a picture of a young soccer player with both arms raised towards the crowd. The headline said LET THE GAMES BEGIN ALREADY. When I asked Keith if he'd design this chapter he said, "Sure. How about we start the type on the last page and read it backwards to page one?"

THE VW PRESENTATION

I went to Ingalls Advertising to work on the Volkswagen account. It was breakthrough creative for the 1960s, and remains one of the best bodies of work ever created in the advertising genre. Maybe in any genre.

I know, because I worked on it. And learned more about writing than in my four years in college, where I was an English major.

Arthur Ingalls was a crony of either Hansen or MacPhee, owners of the Hansen–MacPhee Volkswagen dealership, the New England VW distributor. Hence, Ingalls was the only shop outside of Doyle Dane, which did all the national advertising and most of the regional, to enjoy a piece of the account.

My job, if I cared to accept it, was to emulate the style of Doyle Dane's work for the New England VW dealers.

Cared to accept it? I'd have killed for it. There wasn't a copywriter in the world that couldn't become a star by working on that account. It was so fluent. So easy.

So in order to work on VW, I went to work for Ingalls.

Besides Volkswagen I worked on every other account in the shop. And tried to make ads for them every bit as creative as VW's. Even though some of the products weren't that glamorous.

One such was Marson Klick-Fast Rivets. Klick, with a K. Which may tell us something about how klassy the klient was, and how truly he'd value literary devices like alliteration. Let alone *double entendre*. He was happy with not too many misspellings.

So imagine his delight when I wrote an installation manual ("How to Save Time and Money on Your Next Aluminum Siding Job") in heroic couplets. It was sort of a comic book, only with photos instead of cartoons, showing how you could fasten your four-foot sheets of aluminum to the studding "quick 'n' easy" with Klick-Fast Rivets and captions like:

Insert the rivet in the hole,
That's the Marson Klick-Fast goal!

Blackie Cooper, the Klick-Fast ad manager, and his cigar, were at the presentation, along with Joe Hoffman and Joe Maynard, the owners of Ingalls. There to pump me up. Show some solidarity.

Okay, Ray. Time to rock and roll.

I went front and center, holding up the layouts for Blackie to admire. Blackie didn't applaud. Maybe I was holding them upside-down. Maybe he was just waiting for later, after I'd read the copy. Which I started in doing. Ahem:

It only takes a single click
To hang that siding really quick.

Blackie Cooper and his cigar looked at me. With ineffable admiration. Clearly a connoisseur of language. The Joes, who hadn't had time to look at the work before the presentation, would be proud of me, too. On a roll, I went on, putting some emotion in my voice. A little tremolo.

Through the sheets of tin or plaster,
You'll be thought of as a master.

You'll make your markup u tidy sum,
When you install aluminum!

I ask you, how many writers could find a rhyme for "aluminum"? In the right iambic meter. I could think of nothing that rhymes with "rivet." Other than "privet," and I couldn't find a handy way to work that in.

Blackie Cooper's cigar had gone out. He stared down at the rug. He stared up at Joe Hoffman. There was a catch in his voice. When he said, "Tell me Joe. Tell me as a friend. Ain't this shit?"

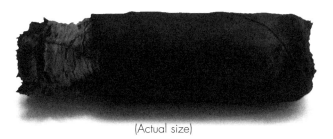

(Actual size)

My first presentation to VW was a month later. Two ads and a billboard. To John Dowd, Jr., marketing manager for Hansen–MacPhee. Who said, as I was wrapping up, "Hey, let's go to lunch."

Both of the Joes got up to join us. But John said, "No offense, guys, but Ray and I just met, and maybe we go out, just the two of us, catch a hot dog, get to know each other."

That said, John and I walked out to the parking lot. He climbed on the back of my motorcycle and we drove to Park Square, a dive where the hot dogs weren't rancid, all you could say about the place. He clinked my beer glass with his and said he hoped this would be a great relationship, as he liked me and thought I had a lot of talent.

"Your ads are funny," he said. "Like Doyle Dane's."

I nodded.

"And they're well-written. You're going to be a good one."

I nodded again.

"But they're wrong," he said. "They're all wrong."

"What do you mean?" I said.

"I mean they suck," he explained.

I was starting to feel glad the Joes weren't here to share my triumph.

"Have you read all the Volkswagen ads? All the ads ever written?"

"No."

"Then I'll get you copies of them. All of them. You read them, you'll learn something."

I did, and I did.

Every ad was 100 words, give or take. Without a single one wasted. The ads were self-deprecating, sometimes funny, but you could never see them crank up a joke, never see from three graphs away that they were priming the pump for a knee-slapping "kicker" (the last line of body copy, which recalled the headline) the way you could with mine. The copy was spare. It told a separate story in every ad, yet never deviated from the story they told in every ad: 20 miles a gallon, seldom needs oil, never needs water, 50,000 miles to a set of tires, no expensive model changes year after year.

How many times can you tell the same story and make it interesting? As many times as Doyle Dane Bernbach told a Volkswagen ad.

Think small. Lemon. Ugly. And on and on.

It's some of the best short-short prose ever written. Including O. Henry and Hemingway. Especially including Poe and Hawthorne, spendthrifts of syllables.

On a good day Twain and Thurber were as good.

But as masters of the language, the structure, the ear, the timing, the economy, the humanity, Doyle Dane Bernbach ought to be taught alongside Shakespeare.

And I'm not kidding.

Circa 1963: my first Volkswagen ad (that actually ran).

Art Direction / Tom McCarthy

THE KILLINGTON PITCH

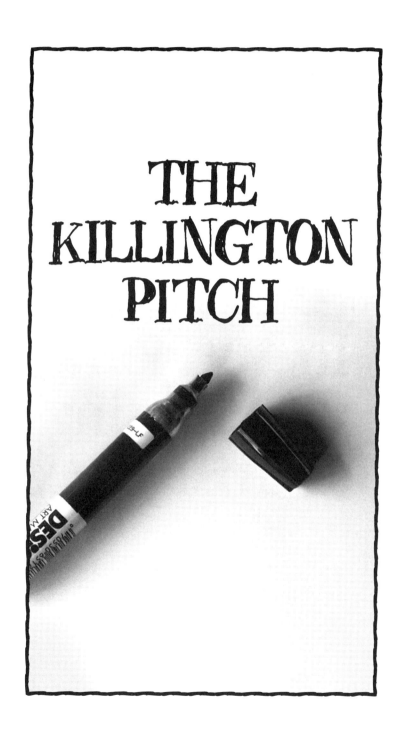

Killington Basin, the ski resort in Vermont, was looking for an agency.

Joe Maynard found this out from a space rep, on a Thursday.

The problem was, if we wanted to be in the pitch, we needed to show up with something on Friday. Something like a full-blown creative presentation. Due tomorrow, nine o'clock, with a five-hour drive to Vermont.

"Can you pull it off, Ray? Make it happen?"

There was no money to be made on the Killington account. But there was free skiing. Joe Maynard was a skier. Joe was president of Ingalls. The answer was swift.

"Sure," I said. In the tone of voice that meant, "How high?"

I walked over to Willy's office, balanced my beer on his art board, and told him we wouldn't be getting much sleep tonight. Milt Wuilleumier, Willy, was my co-creative director. He ran the art side, I ran the copy side. Willy had an assistant, a wrist, who did comps. My side had a staff of one. Which included me.

We went to work.

It was dawn before we had
enough stuff to show. A dozen
half-decent layouts, full-color,
Magic Marker, mounted on heavy
Bainbridge Board, typed copy
pasted down on the back of
the boards.
                Margie Slater,
    our media director,
  had also been up all
    night. Partly
     working out
     the media plan,
   the magazine buy,
   and partly trying to
  figure out how we
 were going to get to
Vermont by nine in the
morning.
    THIS morning.

She found us a way. Bless her, she found us a helicopter.

It would pick us up at Hanscom Field just outside Boston, and set us down in the parking lot at Killington. A five-hour drive compressed to a one-hour flight. What could be bad?

I'll tell you what could be bad. For openers, Joe Maynard was terrified of flying. While the rest of us might fly to, say, New York or

Chicago for a meeting or a presentation, Joe drove. Honest to God, if we'd had a presentation in Los Angeles, Joe would have driven his Chevy before setting foot on a plane.

So imagine his delight when I told him we were going by helicopter.

"Hey, they'll be impressed, Joe. Show them we care enough about the business to rent a helicopter. Bet you nobody else shows up in a chopper."

Not one of Joe's favorite words, I realized.

As it turns out there were other reasons nobody else would show up in a chopper, but more about that later.

"Oh, fuck me," said Joe. "Fuck me, fuck me, fuck me."

But two hours
later he walked
into the aircraft,
the chopper,
like a brave
little boy, and
strapped himself
into one of
the Bell's rear
seats, alongside
Margie, with
sweat pouring
down his face
and his arm-pits
torrenting.

I sat in the front, in the bow,
next to the pilot, a dashing young
man named Bugsy or something.
You had to shout to be heard
over the astonishing noise of the

engine. You've heard the expression "louder than a boiler room"? I have never been in a boiler room, nor do I even know how loud one is, but believe me when I tell you this damn helicopter was louder than any boiler room.

I yelled back to Joe, "HOW YOU DOING?" At the top of my lungs.

"WHAT? WHAT'S THAT?"

"NEVERMIND."

"HUH?"

So you can understand why Joe heard nothing of the conversation I was having with Bugsy somewhere over New Hampshire. (I'll eighty-six the capital letters. But remember we're screaming at each other, me and Bugsy.)

"So Bugsy, aren't
these things
dangerous? Choppers?
I mean, to fly?"

"Whaddaya mean
dangerous?"

"I mean in an
airplane, you know,
with wings, if like
the engine conked
out you could at
least glide down and
land in a field.
Or a road. Maybe not
get killed."

"Nah, engine ever
blows I'd rather be in
this thing. Auto-gyro."

"What?"

"Auto-gyro. Engine blows, you drop like a cinder block 200 feet, then the props start turning by their own self and you land so easy you won't break an egg."

"No shit," I said.

"Here," said Bugsy. "I'll show you."

And he reached over and turned off the engine.

And we dropped like a cinder block 200 feet.

And Joe Maynard screamed so loud we could hear him clearly, even way up here in the bow, before he

threw up all over his blue suit
and the layouts.

And then we're hovering over the ski resort, about to land right in front of the giant window overlooking the parking lot. Behind which sat the seven executives who would sit in judgment of our work and our selves.

In descent, while our aircraft may not break eggs, you should see what it does to those bluestone chips they make parking lots out of. Those stone chips about the size of bullets.

When we were at 50 feet, the first stones just sort of lobbed up there against the glass.

"Plink."

By the time we were at ground level, with the propellers' backwash howling at tornado force, the shards were flying like they were shot from Gatling guns.

"Bang, boing, boom."

Ricocheting. Whistling as they flew. Bugsy waving at a young woman hiding behind a bench, trying to shield her dog from flying rock.

The pane in the picture window cracked. Again and again. The rocks making spider web patterns in the glass. Pedestrians fled. Someone drove a Ford into the woods. For a moment frozen in time I saw, can still see, whenever I'm feverish, a man behind the window, a middle-age citizen wearing a tie, his mouth agape like the person silently screaming in the Munch painting.

There are many reasons
an agency might not
win a piece of business.
But I'll bet you
this is as good as most.

Art Direction / Tom Simons

MY TV DEBUT

Video	Audio

CU of talent holding shoe

THESE DAYS

my voice is commonplace on New England radio and TV, mostly reading commercials I've written myself, for myself to read. Partly because I read my own stuff pretty well, and partly because it pays.

CU of talent holding shoe

You get about $300.- for a local radio spot, double for a TV voiceover, quintuple or more for a spot that runs nationally, and cash the same check again every 13 weeks the commercial airs. It takes about ten minutes to record a spot. (At least when I'm the writer and director as well as the talent.) It's easy work. You don't even have to stand up.

CU of talent holding shoe

But the first time in front of a microphone can be terrifying. Let alone in front of a camera. To this day I

Video	Audio

Still get mike-fright, and update my prescription for tranqs, which I use prophy-lactically maybe a dozen times a year, before a recording session, to quell the panic.

CU of talent holding shoe

If you're ever thrust in front of a microphone, for God's sake don't think of how the larynx or the thorax works. Or the billions of synaptic junction boxes in the brain that email instructions from the eye to the tongue and deliver gibberish to all your many voices and scream at you in unison, in different languages, most of them Scandinavian, when you try to pronounce "Say, folks, speaking of good deals..." and it comes out "Schplik, frogs, smeresh of Goodyear..." This will drive you to tranqs. Same as me.

Video	Audio

CU of talent holding shoe

BUT I DIDN'T

know that then. Back when there was no announcer available to read the three TV spots we had to produce, live, for Knapp Shoes, the night of the Princeton game.

CU of talent holding shoe

Bill Bradley and the Princeton basketball team had won a place in the NCAA semifinals. the president of Knapp Shoes was a Princeton guy. Ingalls Advertising was Knapp's agency. I was the copywriter on the account.

CU of talent holding shoe

YOU can see the domino effect. How I ended up in the studio with three scripts I'd written that morning, got approval for that afternoon, and found no announcer there that night at

Video	Audio

eight o'clock, at the first break in the game, when the first spot for Knapp Shoes was supposed to air.

CU of talent holding shoe

I had on a black suit. The pants had a hole in them, a cigarette burn around the right thigh. You could see white skin showing through. You couldn't miss it. You would say, "Jesus, look at how white that skin is."

The cameraman had an idea. He had a felt-tip marker. Black.

CU of talent holding shoe

Yes. We Magic-Markered my thigh.

CU of talent holding shoe

Video	Audio

And just in time, too. Because the director was counting down, "Four, three, two, rolling," and the red light on the camera was blinking, and the script girl was holding up the cue cards, laboriously chalked on the back of black Bainbridge layout boards.

//////////////////////////////

And then knocked them over. Onto the floor. Like dumping a deck of cards.

//////////////////////////////

CU of talent holding shoe

CU of talent holding shoe

30-second TV spots, of which these three were typical, contain about 80 words. The Lord's Prayer, contains about 60. Which gives you some idea. The "Our Father," and then some, scattered all over the floor on half-a-dozen heavy pieces of cardboard.

Video	Audio
CU of talent holding shoe	**AND ME** standing in front of the camera, live, holding up a shoe.
CU of talent holding shoe	That was my prop. My only one. A size 16-EEEE Knapp Shoe with a steel toe to protect you at work, soft leather insole for comfort at home, and a million people with their eyes glued to me. To my Magic-Markered thigh. Hanging on what I was about to say. Which was this: "Frambish."
CU of talent holding shoe	You too can be a voiceover.

Art Direction / Anthony Henriques

He was my first hire.
I needed another copywriter,
besides myself, and I persuaded
the Joes to let me let the word out.

The first person to show
up was Jay Hill, who would later
be a founder of Hill Holliday.

Jay spoke in lockjaw.
Harvard. Not put on. Not some
wannabe. Turns out his whole
family spoke that way, speaks that
way still, even his kids, to this
day. The most emotional he ever
got, was "Mmmm."

I looked at his book.
I thought it was good. I said so.

"**H**ow much would it take to
get you to come here?" I asked
him.

He replied, "Mmmm."
In lockjaw. "How much are you
offering?"

"**J**ay, I don't have a budget.
Gotta sell you to the Joes. Name
me a figure and I'll try and get it
for you."

"Mmmm," he said.

This went on for ten minutes, Jay unable to mention a dollar amount. It wasn't something one discussed. I'm sure that's one of the big reasons that a few years later he opened his own shop.

The next person to show up was Corso Donati, who said immediately that he played the tenor saxophone and needed $14,000.

He was worth it. Even though I was only making $12,000 at the time. Which disparity I had a tough time justifying to the Joes.

"I want this guy," I said. "You can make it up to me later, when the agency can afford it."

(Which they did.)

So Corso moved in with me, into my big white office, where we both pounded on manual typewriters and smoked non-filter Camels, which were the only kind of Camels they made in those days, and laughed a whole lot. Donati had one of those laughs, the easy adjective for which is "infectious." Which would be like calling Typhoid Mary "infectious" if she coughed in your face. If Corso laughed, you laughed. It was that simple. And we did so an awful lot, there in our white office with the walls turning yellow from the smoke from our two packs a day of Camels. Each.

One day Harold Turin, a reformed cigarette smoker, came into our office carrying cures. He came bearing a box of cigars, two corncob pipes (which require no breaking in), and a five-pound tin of pipe tobacco.

It said on the label: "Barking Dog (Never Bites)."

"Here," said Harold, "smoke these. Cigars, pipes. Get you off those freaking cigarettes." Harold was our friend and truly loved us.

After a week, Corso and I were up to five cigars a day and five pipefuls of Barking Dog (Never Bites), which we inhaled. Plus the same two packs of Camels, each, and the walls were getting yellower and yellower.

"En boca lupa," Corso would say. "In the mouth of the wolf." Italian for "if you are about to be eaten by a wolf, then look the sucker in the mouth," if not the eye. I don't know why. Me, I'd rather cower, run, look away, hunch down, anything but look the wolf in the mouth. But Corso would say, "En boca lupa."

"En

So be it. If my fate is to be eaten by a wolf, here in Rhode Island, I'll look him in the mouth. Pissing in my pants, but looking him right square in the freaking mouth.

That year, I won seven Hatch bowls, the New England award for "Creative Excellence in Advertising." Corso won an Honorable Mention, a 10-1/2" x 14" piece of paper saying "nice going." but it was worth hanging on the wall. Everyone did so. Corso hung his Hatch award over his desk. It was cute.

It got even cuter. Because every week Harold would come in and trot the award over to the Photostat machine and reduce it by a few percent. After a month he had it shrunk to 9" x 12". Another month, down to 8-1/2" x 11".

boca

CORSO

Corso never noticed.

Until Harold, in frustration one night, reduced it to 3" x 5". The size of an index card. And the next day, at coffee time, Corso gazed up the wall. And you could hear him laugh from a block away. Harold and me holding our stomachs. Corso flapping this stupid little index card, his first Hatch award, tears rolling down his eyes.

A few years later Corso was at Massachusetts General Hospital, with lung cancer. Hooked up to tubes. When I went to see him, I said, "How you doing, pal?"

He said, "God, I'd give anything for a Camel.

I lit one up, for both of us. "Give me a nickel," I said.

lupa"

We smoked for a few minutes and talked about the business and then about personal things and made our peace. Two days later he died. (Probably the Camel.)

But not before I told him, "En boca lupa, brother. Look that sucker right in the mouth."

And while you're at it, laugh at the bastard.

And not before the Director of the Ad Club came to his bedside and presented Corso with a silver Revere Bowl, a week before the ceremonies. (A Revere Bowl is a top Hatch Award, one you can't trot to the stat machine under the cover of darkness and reduce by millimeters every night. One that doesn't turn yellow from two people smoking cigarettes and cigars and pipes of Barking Dog [Never Bites] in one shared office.)

The service was held at a chapel in Forest Hill Cemetery near the trolley tracks. Stan Getz played saxophone through speakers overhead. Half the creatives in Boston advertising were there. I sat in a back pew between Harold Turin and Carl Casselman.

Corso's estranged wife catered the affair. One reason she was estranged is that she and Corso had absolutely nothing in common. Corso smoked, drank, told bawdy stories and laughed. She, on the other hand, could tell you about chakras.

To perform the service she brought in her guru, an Indian preacher. Or maybe he was Pakistani. He spoke for nearly an hour before we realized he was speaking English. We were starting to catch a few words now and again, about one's soul flying to de sky.

Close by, a trolley rumbled past, so loudly that you couldn't hear the preacher over the basso din. Harold whispered, "The hell is that?"

CORSO

And in that peaceful pause, that sweet moment of silence between the soul flying off to de sky and de train clattering away in de distance, Casselman stage-whispered, so the whole chapel could hear it.

"**T**hat's Corso. Rolling over."

Design / Dave Lizotte
Art / Larry Bagley
Illustrations / Mark Bellerose

After eight years, I left Ingalls Advertising to start a freelance practice.

Alexander Brodsky, owner of a tiny agency a few blocks down on Newbury Street, was a long-time fan of my work, and wanted to talk to me about working for him.

"Alex, I can give you a couple, three days a week, but no more. My aim is to work with my own accounts."

"Give me three days a week. For a year. Build me a Creative department. Win me some awards. Then go do whatever the hell you want. But give me a year." We agreed.

My first job was to find us a good art director. Of the many people who showed up for interviews, Jimbo was the best.

Also the biggest. Over six feet, close to 300 pounds, and man, could he sweat. Especially the day he came for the interview, a 90-degree day in August when the elevator was down and he had to schlep his portfolio up three flights of stairs. You could have wrung out his suit coat. He showed me about 50 pieces of work, 25 of which were adequate.

The other 25 were sensational.

"How much you looking for, Jimbo?"

"Ten grand. That's what they were paying at Hill Holliday." Before they fired him.

"Can you start on Monday?"

"Yeah. See you then."

And he packed up his samples and clomped down the stairwell.

"Who was that large, sweaty person?" said Alex.

"That's our new art director," I said.

That's how their relationship began, and then it got worse. From cat–dog it went to mongoose–cobra.

JIMBO

It got to the point where I drew a chalk-mark on the floor, a line in the sand, and told Alex that on this side of the line was the Creative department and nobody could cross it without my permission. Not him, not Gloria the account executive, whom Jimbo was starting to loathe even more than Alex, not anyone. And Jimbo, you don't cross the line in the other direction. Is that clear? Everyone? You got it? Okay, back to your desks. Now.

I have never seen such instant mutual antipathy among human beings as between Jimbo and Alex and Gloria. And it kept festering like a giant boil that would some-day have to be lanced, and then watch out. Duck.

In fairness to Alex and Gloria, I admit that Jimbo had habits that management, even the sanest of us, might have second thoughts about. Like his tendency to drift into the office by the tick of his own biological clock.

"Where the fuck you been?" I would query, inviting discussion.

"Sorry, Ray, I had to wash the car."

And that would be that. I really didn't give a damn when he came or went. Far as I was concerned, his work was wonderful, keeping up with the same ratio of strikeouts-to-homers he displayed in his portfolio. But Alex and Gloria had a slightly different per-spective on things. And you could sense things building up, if you noticed the size of people's carotid arteries when they talked to you about their large, sweaty employees.

One morning at 10 o'clock our receptionist buzzed me and said, "Ray, you've got a call on line two."

"Who is it," I said.

"I think it's Jimbo speaking with a Spanish accent."

Sure enough it was Jimbo speak-ing with a Spanish accent. He said, "Thees ees me."

"Where the hell are you?" I in-quired.

"You need me today?"

"Well, today's a workday, you know?"

"Listen, man, you need me I can be there."

"What is this 'can be' bullshit?"

"You know, if it's desirable for me to be in the office, I can *be* in the office."

"Jimbo, where you calling from, you mind my asking?"

"Daytona." He and a buddy had driven down to watch the stock car races.

Jimbo never lied. At least not to me. That I know of.

Then we got this assignment from Bond Atomic, a client that made ruby lasers and fiber-optic tubing and other high-tech stuff, and they needed a trade show booth. Right up Jimbo's alley. He plunged into designing the booth, which was going to be constructed at the Javits Center in New York or someplace, and he showed up early every morning for the next few days.

At the time, there was an exhibit at one of the art galleries on Newbury Street. A traveling exhibit of sculpture made from tiny fiber-optic tubing. Among other things, fiber-optic wheat fields blowing in the breeze, the

JIMBO

little wheat fronds all a-glow with fiber-transmitted sunlight. A dozen or so works of art. All of which looked best in a room with no other light source.

Jimbo's idea was to rent the entire exhibit and position its components strategically in a light-tight booth the size of a boxcar, along with lasers and other products made by Bond Atomic. Viewers would navigate their way around a pitch-dark maze by way of a velvet-covered rope like you find in a movie theater to keep you from bolting into the seats without paying, and kind of feel their way around corners until they came upon a twinkling fiber-optic wheat field or what-ever.

I loved it. So did Bond. Even Alex and Gloria didn't hate it.

So we rented the whole exhibit from the sculptor, insured it to the hilt, and had it packed in padded boxes to be shipped off to the booth soon to be built for it at the Javits Center.

Jimbo was the only one who knew how the booth should be built. The light-tight boxcar with its maze of winding pas-sageways, sudden turns, and (voila!) revelations. "It's a little tiny *wheat* field, Harry, made outta fiber-optic glass tubing!

JIMBO

See how it glows as the wind blows it! We got to get us some of that tubing from Bond Atomic!" It was going to be boffo.

And Jimbo was going to fly to the Javits Center tomorrow to oversee the construction of his masterpiece. Where a crew of six would be waiting for him at nine o'clock with the twelve padded boxes of priceless sculpture and all the lumber and nails and shit it would take to build the com-plicated corridors of a light-tight maze in a boxcar.

At 9:30 Gloria called me. She said, "Where's Jimbo?"

"Maybe he missed his flight, be on the next one."

He wasn't on it, is what Gloria said when she called me at 10:30. And again at noon. And two o'clock.

"If he's not here by three, fire his sorry ass," she suggested.

So I started making phone calls. To find out where he was. Was he stranded? Was he hurt? Was he dead, what? I called his house, no answer. I called his mother's house; no, she hadn't seen him. I called a couple of his drinking buddies; no, they knew nothing. Then I remembered he used to hang out with a bunch of guys, his home-town cops. So I called the Quincy Police Station, and Patrolman Connell told me, "You a friend of his?"

"Yes, I am," I said. I was. And I am.

"Hang on a second."

Which I did, until a voice came on the line saying, "Who's this?"

"This is Ray. Gloria is some pissed."

"Heh-heh," the voice said.

"Heh."

It is not a wise man—nor woman—who fucks with

JIMBO.

Art Direction / Jim Sinatra

Where the canary kept dying

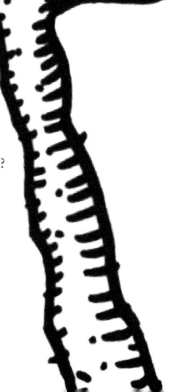

Larry Miller lured me into partnership, with promises of staggering wealth in the world of show business. Well, not exactly "promises." Mostly just allusions. To his friends in show business, like Stephen Sondheim. "If you need a track for a show you're writing, I guess I could ask Stevie to do one for you." Like that.

And not exactly "show business." Unless you mean industrial slide shows. Yes, there was the occasional film, but most of the work we did was with 35mm slides. Sometimes with a whole bunch of projectors that had to be programmed on punched tape, synched up, capable of all kinds of mischief. One bulb blows, the whole show goes down. One glitch in the tape, the show goes down.

You haven't lived unless you've spent weeks writing and producing a multi-media show, and there are 5,000 people in the audience, including the client, who hasn't paid you yet, and the lights dim, the music comes up, and a projector goes down.

I, at least, have lived.

And damn near died.

Because of a bulb.

And the part about "staggering wealth"? I should have caught on when I first saw the office. It was ground-floor space in the Motor Mart Garage building. Above the studio were eight cement floors paved with parked cars.

Did you know carbon monoxide sinks? I didn't either.

We had a receptionist name of Yogi. Pretty French-Canadian woman with a heart of gold, a tongue of silver, and an ear of tin. Her diction was impeccable. It was always with precision that she'd pick up the phone and enunciate, "My ass who's calling, please?"

One day Art Garfunkel came by to visit Larry. From my office next to the reception area this is what I heard:

"I'm here to see Mr. Miller, please."

"Jewish Sam or Larry?" (Sam and Larry are both named Miller.)

"I guess I would wish Larry."

"My ass who's here to see him?"

"Art Garfunkel."

"Who you witch?"

"Beg pardon?"

"What company."

"Simon and Garfunkel."

"He suspecting you?"

"Yes, I have an appointment."

Yogi buzzed Larry.

"Larry, there's a Mr. Garfinkle to see you."

"Who?"

"From Simmons and Garfinkle?"

Oh, God, I loved Yogi.

And hey, if I couldn't get Stevie Sondheim to do me a track, maybe I could get this Garfinkle guy. Who knew.

Art Direction / Bill Murphy

My Letterhead

I opened up shop at the top floor
of the Hotel Bradford, close to
Boston's Combat Zone, along with
a bunch of other freelancers. It
was sort of a commune. We called
it The Roof.

There was a gaggle of graphic
design studios with upscale names
(like "Flyspecks"), an illustrator,
photographer John Goodman, some
audio-visual producers, and a guy
who answered the telephone who
turned out to be a CIA agent.
Why, I don't know. But there he
sat, at the front desk, wearing a

sport coat and
tie, surrounded
by weirdoes
with tattoos
and earrings,
and freelance
writers like
me.

The ceiling of
my office was

peeling so badly that I strung
a yellow parachute from it
and worked under the strange
diffused light, and loved
it.

John Murray stopped by.

"I'm back from California,
man" he said, "and I need
some work."

Until he left for the
Coast, John Murray had been
the enfant terrible of Boston
advertising. The bad boy
art director who had won
a bunch of awards for
his in-your-face ads and
posters. One of his posters
was for a play called Riot! It
was a theater event that warned
about what our prevailing race
relations could lead to. After
the posters were printed he
burned the edges of some and
shot bullet holes through
the rest, and stuck them up
all over town on telephone poles
and sides of phone booths. To

hint at what could happen. Subtle
bastard, Murray. I was a fan.

Clean-cut, he'd left Boston for
Hollywood, where he went to design
movie posters. He came back with
long hair
wearing a
black beard
and biker
boots. I
was happy
to see him.

"I'll do
anything for a hundred bucks," he
said, sitting under the parachute,
drinking a can of my beer.

"Johnny, I got nothing for you. Just
starting out, got no work. No clients yet."

He thought for a moment.

"You got your own corporate I.D. yet?
Letterhead, business cards, all that?"

"No," I said.

"You will. Just give me a hundred bucks."

Done deal.

He called me the next
day and said, "I got
something for you."

"Good."

"But you won't have the balls to buy it."

"Try me," I said.

So he came over and showed it to
me. The letterhead. It was "Ray
Welch Associates" done in squiggles.
Ballpoint pen, as if someone had
doodled it, on a yellow legal pad,
the kind I carried with me to take
notes on at client meetings, the
kind I wrote first-draft copy on. There
was probably nothing more emblematic
of me at the time,
pre-word processor
days, than a yellow pad
and a ballpoint pen.
(Well actually, I used
a #1 pencil, but ball
point blue looked
better against a
canary-yellow background.)

It was the funkiest corporate
I.D. ever designed.

"Sold," I said. "Give me a
mechanical."

In those days, a "mechanical"
is what you printed from.
Camera-ready artwork from which
the printer made a plate and
printed the stuff. These days
everything is on film or disk,
usually just scanned from a
computer to the printing press;
but back then you gave the
printer a mechanical, a piece
of Bainbridge Board with the
so-called "finished artwork"
pasted down on it.

John Murray gave me a mechanical.
Because it was a two-color job
(blue squiggles for the header
and blue horizontal lines on
the paper, plus the red vertical
line that runs down the left
margin of legal pads), the

mechanical came with two sheets of
clear plastic overlays, separations,
"seps" for each layer of plastic
for its own color.

I called Lee Daniels, owner of
Daniels Press, a printer who did a
lot of high-end work for advertising
agencies. Brochures, annual
reports. A month
ago I'd given
Daniels a fancy
brochure to
print, a 12-page
book for a
client of mine,
a real estate
development on
the Cape, six-color plus varnish,
expensive, so he sort of owed me one.

"Lee," I said on the phone, "I've got
some I.D. for myself, needs printing."

"No charge," he said.

"No way," I said, setting down
the rules we'd play by for years to
come. "Just go easy on me." And
he said he'd be over my place

around four o'clock, maybe have a beer with me.

"So, Ray," he said, glass in hand, "You got a mechanical?"

I handed it to him. Complete with seps. He looked at it.

"Uh, you got some idea what typeface you want here?" He pointed to the squiggles that said Ray Welch Associates. "Maybe a nice clean Helvetica? Or something classic like a Century or a Goudy?"

"That's the mechanical, Lee," I said.

He looked at me fatherly, kindly.

"You don't understand, Ray. You're a writer, don't expect you to know a lot about production. But I got to tell you, if this were an actual mechanical, this is how the stuff would actually look."

Lee left the bar shaking his head.

The other half of the people in
the world, the half I had it
printed for, actually got it. The
letterhead won a first, a Revere
bowl, in the Hatch Awards, in the
Corporate Identity category.

Value? The whole thing cost me a
hundred bucks.

Go figure.

Art Direction and Illustrations / Karen Lynch

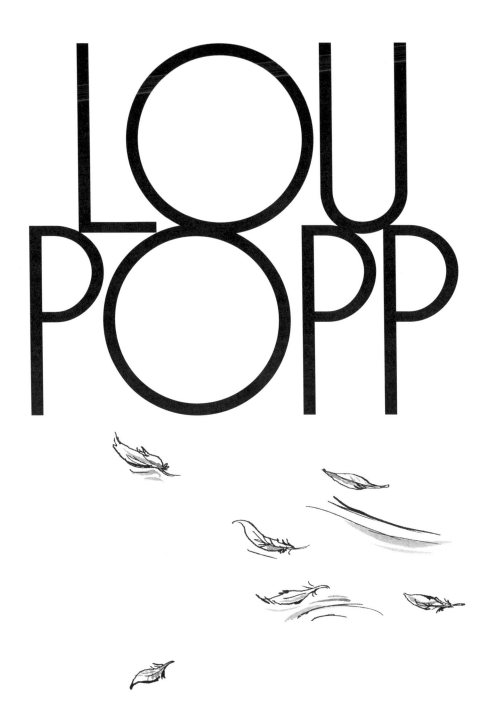

He was a writer Gail and I would hire from time to time, and sometimes traded for a left-handed art director or a player to be named later. "Hey, Ray, we need a writer for a week or two, can you spare Lou Popp?"

"**M**aybe. You got any Celtics tickets?"

His credentials, when he came looking for work, included writing for the Pure One Chicken account, which had won a bunch of heavy-duty creative awards.

"**Y**ou work on the television?" I asked.

"**N**o."

"**T**he radio?"

"**N**o."

"**T**he hell you work on, then?"

"**W**ing tags."

"**T**he what?"

"**T**he wing tags."

"**Y**ou mean those little tags they staple to the wings? Of the dead chickens?"

"**Y**es. Those wing tags."

He was a handsome guy, Harvard grad, smart enough, good writer, who cashed in on his air of melancholy. Used it to pick up chicks.

"Woe is me," he would say, and tell how his wife had left him, and he lost his job, and he was genetically destined to die young. And the girl would go home with him.

Some men envied his pitifulness.

Once we were working on a Presidential race, for Birch Bayh, and we were writing a film to use as a fundraiser in the New Hampshire primary. Supposed to be a documentary. Everything true.

Instead (surprise!), we staged an event, with twenty-odd people in a room, a representative cross-section of New Hampshire's population. Rich folk, poor folk, one black guy.

There is an old tune, from the 1800s, when they were laying track across the country, called "The Gandy Dancers' Ball," which goes like this:

> *A gandy dancer is a railroad man,*
> *And his work is never done.*
> *With his pick and shovel and his willing hand,*
> *He makes the railroad run.*

For the Bayh fundraiser film, we cast Lou as an out-of-work railroad employee. A laid-off gandy dancer. Looking mournful, he spoke to the camera. "Senator Bayh, I've been out of work near six months now, from the railroad. Which if there were more of them would be good for this great country. If I vote for you, how will you help me?"

And Lou was so pitiable that people would believe it. "Poor damn gandy dancer," they would say, looking at our documentary, looking at Lou Popp's dark eyes. His willing hand.

"**O**ut of work for six months." Poor freaking gandy dancers. Birch Bayh, by God, would do something about that. When elected. Especially about those good-looking Harvard-educated gandy dancers like Lou Popp.

And Birch would tell us how he would help, and then play the piano and sing "Way Back Home in Indiana," and the voters would jump on board.

Lou used his pitiability to the hilt, all the time. Which used to piss off Gail. "Listen, you asshole," she would console, "you're a little short, but you're a young, handsome guy. With adequate talent. Making decent money. So stop your whining."

I have lived with Gail for over a quarter of a century. In case you wondered what keeps me from self-pity.

So Lou calls the office one morning just after nine. And says, "Ray, you mind if I don't come in today?"

"What's up, Lou?"

"Got into a car accident. My BMW. On Memorial Drive." Memorial is the beltway road that runs along the Charles River on the Cambridge side, paralleling Storrow Drive on the Boston side. Lou said he was reaching for a smoke, a pack of cigarettes that had drifted over to the passenger side of the dash, and pulled the steering wheel as he did so, and steered the BMW into an aluminum lamppost, which won. "Got banged up some."

"You drunk, Lou?" I said, showing the compassion I learned from Gail. "You sound awful."

"No," he went on.

"Then I'm coming over, see how you're doing." And Gail and I got into my two-seat Fiat Spider and drove to Lou's duplex in Cambridge. Where he came out of the door with what looked like a Coke bottle sticking out of his forehead. Pieces of windshield.

"You been to the hospital, man?"

"Yeah, St. Elizabeth's."

"Well, let's go back there. I think they missed a little."

They'd missed about a pint bottle's worth. Lou was there for an hour while a doctor plucked shards of spidery safety glass out of his head. After which we all squeezed into the Fiat and started driving him back to Cambridge.

"Would you mind," Lou said weakly, "would you mind stopping at Stadium Auto Body, where they towed my car, and let me have a look? It's almost on the way."

"Let's have a look," I said.

We stopped outside the fence, where the attendant said to Lou, "You were in that freaking car? The BMW? Someone actually survived that wreck? Walked away?"

Then we saw why he said that.

Lou's car was parked—actually it was laying down on its side, dead—in the back lot. Where the totals were heaped. There is no way a human being could have left that car alive. It was crumpled. With a shorn-off aluminum lamppost sticking straight through the driver's seat.

To get to the back lot you had to pass through a gate in the cyclone fence, a four-foot gap guarded by two chained junkyard dogs, a German Shepherd and a Doberman, both growling and salivating, so you had to walk right in the middle of the gap in the fence to keep from being torn apart. We marched single-file, hands at our sides. And we walked up to the once-BMW, and Lou said, "Jesus."

He stared at the wreck. "I should have been killed," he said. "I should be dead."

Gail lit in. "There! See, you fool? See how lucky you are? Now do you see how stupid it is for you to whine and complain all the time?"

"You're right," he said, as we turned around and marched back through the opening in the fence. "You're right. I'm invincible!" And he snapped his fingers. Like that.

As he did so, the Doberman bit him in the arm. Dobermans being hard to pry off of people.

We drove him back to St. Elizabeth's for six stitches and a tetanus shot.

Twenty years later, Lou was a creative director with McCann, happily married, father of a baby girl. On a trip to London he suffered a massive heart attack and died an instant, early death.

Nobody was surprised.

But Jesus, we hurt.

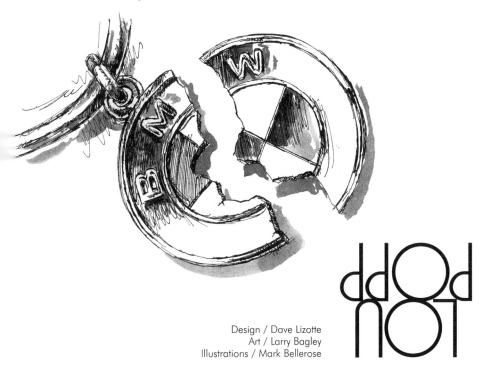

Design / Dave Lizotte
Art / Larry Bagley
Illustrations / Mark Bellerose

THE HAT

At four in
the morning,
my former wife
shook me awake,
screaming

**"Get up!
Get up!
Someone's
being
killed in
the alley!"**

I sat ^{up,} **alert in an instant.**

Sure enough, From the sounds rising up from the alley, someone was being murdered. **"Whack!"**
The sickening sound of ribs being smashed. "Whack!"
Followed by a man's high-pitched wail of "Stop! Stop!"

This wasn't my first brush with violence in the alley. A few months before, trying to break up a fistfight between two old men, one of them blind-sided me with a blackjack, knocking me down and destroying most of the nerves in the right side of my face. Making it tough, for about a year, to eat soup or drink beer without drooling. I was forever trying to shoe away drug dealers, vagrants, and prostitutes of both sexes. I usually kept an eye out for guns or knives but I guess I forgot about blackjacks.

My address, Townsend Place, was an alley off an
alley in Park Square, across from the Trailways
bus station on Carver Street.

The neighborhood was a confluence of harsh sub-
cultures. At the corner of Townsend and Carver
there was a gay bar. Next to it was a restaurant
with an outdoor area that bordered my back door,
where you could hear very clearly the sounds of
people throwing up. A few doors up Carver Street
was Lundin Turkish Baths, a pickup place for rough
trade. Next to the baths was the Hillbilly Ranch,
a bar with loud live cowboy music for guys in boots
and Stetsons and women in leather micro-skirts
often festooned with tasteful touches of turquoise.

Once a month I'd find a ransacked suitcase or a
purse with no money in it, stolen from a transient
at the bus station and chucked into the alley.
Whenever there was identification left, which was
rare, I'd mail it back to the owners, frequently
sweet women from the Midwest vowing never again
to visit Auntie Rose in our devil-ridden Sodom.
Once I got a call from a lady to whom I'd returned
a wallet with a driver's license and Social Security
card.

She was astonished that there was a single decent citizen in all of Boston. May God bless you, sir, and could I send you a ten-dollar reward?

Aside from that kind of stuff, it was a nice little residential neighborhood.

Before they filled in most of the Back Bay, Townsend Place was waterfront property. There were three townhouses on the street, all owned by the city to accommodate out-of-town official visitors. As the area got landfilled, the city grew up and spread out around Townsend Place, gradually turning the area shabby and shadowy.

You'd never know there was a house back there unless you knew the neighborhood. Even the cops didn't know.

One day I came back from a motorcycle trip to find yellow police barriers barring Carver Street, wall to wall with fire trucks. Hoses were being unrolled. Smoke was pouring up from the Hillbilly Ranch, which almost abutted my house.

I weaved the motorcycle between the sawhorses, through the yellow tape, and parked next to the gay bar at the corner of the alley. My front door was open, and hip-booted firefighters were racing in and out. A few Good Samaritans, including my father-in-law, who had been visiting for a few weeks, were lugging furniture and appliances out of the house and securing them in the cellar of a neighboring Chinese restaurant, away from harm.

"Is my house going to burn down?" I shouted at a fireman.

"We don't know yet. Depends on the wind. But, yeah, the chances are pretty good."

THE HAT

I went back for the motorcycle, which was still running.

A policeman grabbed me by the arm and pushed me against a wall. "The hell you think you're doing, mister? You just crossed a police line. I should arrest you right now."

"My house may be burning down."

"What house."

"My house. I live back there. Around the corner. Sort of behind the Hillbilly Ranch."

"There are no houses back there," he enlightened me.

"My house is back there." All the others had long
since been turned into warehouses.

"Listen, asshole, you got ten seconds to get on
that bike and get out of here or you're in jail."

I told him again that I lived back there. That
there was a house back there.

He signaled to another patrolman. They picked me
up by the armpits and threw me into a paddywagon.

Seldom in my life have I felt so frustrated.
Pacing back and forth inside a six—by-ten cell on
wheels. I threw my shoulder at the rear door. Then
I kicked it with all my strength. Don't ever let
anyone tell you American vehicles aren't well made.

Ten minutes later I heard my father-in-law's voice.
A retired Army guy, he knew how to talk to people
in uniforms. He was explaining to the cops that
indeed there was a house back there. That it was
in danger of conflagration.

That the guy locked in the wagon was likely to be in a snit. "He has an attitude about authority," my father-in-law said.

THE HAT

Which I do. Ever since my first grade principal summoned me to his office, and there was a cop there, accusing me of stealing a yo-yo from the local hardware store. Chalk it up to not getting off on the right foot.

Not counting this paddywagon, I've been arrested three times, fingerprinted once, and locked up twice. Including an overnighter in Newport, during a jazz festival. Where dozens of young men had been deputized to help the local police with crowd control.

Meaning tear gas and billyclubs. Young men with
mace and sticks and deputy badges are some of my
favorites.

The cops let me out of the wagon.

In the half-hour I was locked up, the wind had
calmed. The roof of the Hillbilly Ranch was
soaked with water, smoke and steam spritzing
through the shingles.

The house never did burn down. A wrecking ball
razed it a few years later. Park Square is now
home to the Transportation Center, a brick two-
block-long monolith that squats over what used
to be a gay bar, the Hillbilly Ranch, the steam
baths, and Townsend Place.

Where tonight you heard some poor bastard being
beaten with a club and screaming, "Stop! Stop!"

I leapt out of bed, grabbed my pistol from the
bureau, and raced down three flights of stairs.
In the foyer there was a hat rack, used mostly to
hang jackets and windbreakers. Tonight, it also
had a hat hanging on it. An ancient wide-brimmed
fedora. Where this hat came from, I'll never know.

Except for on the
golf course, I
never wear a hat.
Let alone a fedora.
But for whatever
reason, I jammed
it on my head as I
flung open the front
door and ran down
the alley barefoot.
Also bare-ass. Firing my gun in the air, to warn off
the bad guys. And to let the victim know that help
was on the way, I started screaming. **"I'm coming!
I'm coming!"**

And what do I see as I round the corner toward
Carver Street? With my raised gun booming into the
dawn, my festive
fedora jammed down
around my ears, hol-
lering, "I'm coming,
I'm coming"? I see
the trash collectors.
Big blue Department
of Public Works
truck backing into
the alley.

THE
HAT

A DPW guy with a broomstick whacking the trash barrels to scare away the rats. Another guy guiding the truck, making hand signals for the driver to cut the wheels left, or cut the wheels right, or to stop. As in "Stop! Stop!"

I stared at them. Starting to comprehend. They stared at me. Thinking there was nothing much else that needed comprehending about a naked man with a gun yelling that he's coming. Not in *this* neighborhood.

I said, "How do you do?"

The men jumped into the front seat of the truck and they sped away. As much as a dump truck can speed.

The following Tuesday, trash day for Park Square, nobody from the DPW showed up at Townsend Place. Nor the following Tuesday. So I called the Department of Public Works and said I had a problem. That my trash hadn't been picked up. For the second week in a row. A gruff voice said, "Where do you live?"
"Park Square."

"What's the address?"

"Townsend Place."

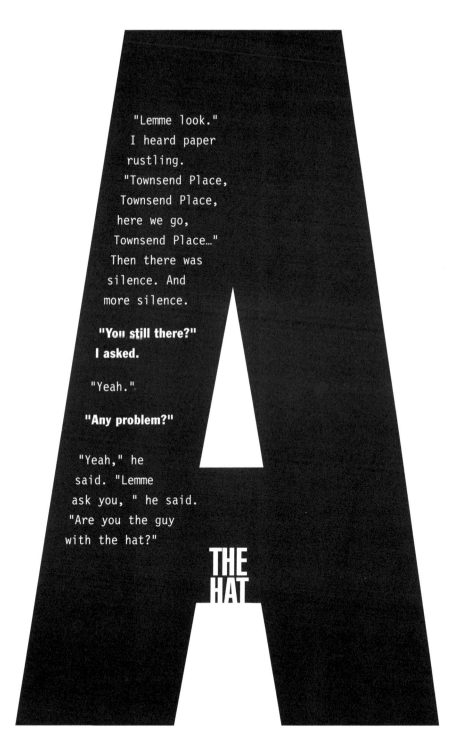

"Lemme look."
I heard paper
rustling.
"Townsend Place,
Townsend Place,
here we go,
Townsend Place…"
Then there was
silence. And
more silence.

**"You still there?"
I asked.**

"Yeah."

"Any problem?"

"Yeah," he
said. "Lemme
ask you, " he said.
"Are you the guy
with the hat?"

THE
HAT

THE HAT ⊥HE THE

Design / Bob Cipriani   Production / Paul Wheeler

The

INTERVIEW

*M*ary Moore was Creative Director at Humphrey Browning MacDougall, which was maybe the best agency ever to happen to Boston until Hill Holliday came along.

Mary Moore was queen of HBM.

*A*t the time she was dating Carl Casselman, one of the best creative directors in Boston, who later went on to become a director of TV commercials. A friend of mine.

One day she was interviewing a young would-be copywriter. She pored over his book, nodding from time to time. Finally she closed the portfolio and addressed the young man.

"Good book. But you made two mistakes."

"First, you stole a lot of Carl Casselman's ads. Plagiarized them.

Second, you didn't steal his best stuff."

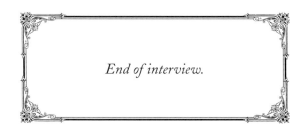

End of interview.

*A*rt direction / Anthony Henriques

THE VOTER EDUCATION PROJECT

In 1976, the year of the Gerry Ford–Jimmy Carter race, a guy named David Levine called, asked if I wanted to help save America.

"Sure," I said. I wasn't busy.

David was with something called the Voter Education Project. It was a thinly veiled arm of the Democratic National Committee. It was trying to get unregistered voters to register, on the theory that most unregistered voters were either poor or minorities or criminally insane and therefore more likely to vote Democrat.

They wanted a TV campaign, persuade folks to register. Which they wanted me to write and produce. But first we had to sell the DNC on a boffo concept, always the hard part.

So, as usual, what I did was dump the problem on Gail. And, as usual, she nailed it.

"The only reason I vote," she said, "is to cancel out my father's vote." Her father, even though an otherwise decent man, is a Republican. And won't go see a priest about it.

So we wrote a campaign that pitted
well-known antagonists against each
other, canceling out each other's vote.
The Great Equalizer.

We wrote scripts for Ali vs. Cosell,
Chico vs. The Man, Archie Bunker vs.
Meathead, and a bunch of others. All
with the message, "You know why I'm
going to vote, you asshole? Because
you're going to vote."

It was a smart campaign, but I
thought it would never fly. Because you
don't just call up Mohammed Ali and
say, "Hey, how about being in a Public
Service Announcement? There's no money
in it, but it will maybe get you some
publicity." Or call up Carroll O'Connor
and say, "Hey, you want to be on TV?"

That's what most clients would
tell you. "Nice idea, Ray, but it can't
be done." What David Levine said is,
"Nice idea, Ray, let's go do it."

Turns out one of the people on the
Democratic National Committee was the
then-Mrs. Norman Lear, wife of the pro-
ducer of All in the Family and several
other TV shows. Somebody else on the
DNC had an in with Freddie Prinze.
Somebody else was actually tight with
Ali. Etc.

And we did it. With all those folks.

The first shoot was with Ali and Howard Cosell, at a sound stage in Chicago. Ali entered with an entourage of about twenty people. Women dressed in white robes, bodyguards, sycophants, and Don King. A stream of people, all marching behind Mohammed Ali, the most famous man in the world.

And not to be intimidated.

We sat at a table in back, away from the crowd, to go over the script. I had written something like this:

COSELL: Say, Champ, are you a registered voter?

ALI: What do you think I am, a chump?

So I played Cosell, reading his lines, and started walking Ali through his part, going to give him some direction. Tell him how to play the heavyweight champion.

"I'll be Howard, you be you," I said, handing him a script. "Here we go." I tried to sound like Cosell. "Say, Champ, are you a registered voter?"

He read from the script, haltingly, "What do you think I am, a chomp?"

At the time, Ali was a demigod. But he was also functionally illiterate. At least that's how it looked to me. Don't sue me, Champ.

So I took away the script, fed him his lines, and we went through it orally, me doing Cosell, Ali doing Ali.

By the third walk-through he had it down. Pat.

It was Cosell, who refused any pre-shoot direction, who blew the first two takes. Even so, we had it in three.

A few weeks later I worked again with Ali, this time in the Poconos, where he was training for the Norton fight. We flew in at night, during a lightning storm, pitching and yawing, in a little tiny Cessna with 35mm cameras strapped to the wings. Strapping 100-pound cameras to the wings does not enhance the flying experience.

My friend, photographer John Goodman came along, partly to take publicity shots, partly because, as a serious photographer and serious boxing fan, he wanted to do a study of Ali. He shot dozens of rolls of film, mostly of the Champ training, working out. As a bonus,

Floyd Patterson and Ruben "Hurricane" Carter were ringside, watching the training, and John got pictures of them, up close and personal.[1] He shot 100 photos of me working with Ali, during the shoot and also just horsing around. Me holding the heavy bag for him, for example. Me arm wrestling with him. Me and Ali.

AND JOHN LOST ALL THE FILM

At least until 20 years later, when he was cleaning out a closet and found a single shot of me and the most famous man in the world.

I have one picture, one stinking 5"x7" photograph, of me and Ali[2]. We're looking at a clipboard, going over a script, Ali wearing a white robe, overhead mike cutting off my forehead. It's in a little frame, sitting on my piano, and it's captioned: Ray Teaches Him the Rope-a-Dope.

---

[1]Goodman e-mailed me this: "After I finished shooting Ali, I stepped down from the ring and was face to face with both of them. Shyness has never been my strong suit so I quickly reached out to both of them to introduce myself and shake their hands. Much to my embarrassment when I shook Hurricane's hand (who was out of jail awaiting a re-trial thanks to Bob Dylan in which he was again wrongly convicted) it seemed like every bone cracked creating what I felt was a loud embarrassing noise. Now flash forward to January 1999 and I am working on the set of the movie "The Hurricane" starring Denzel Washington. Carter was on the set as an advisor and my first day I had lunch with Ruben who had been given my book. We talked boxing... and then I told him I had met him at Ali's training camp in 1976 and that I had been so mortified by that noisy handshake. Of course he had no recollection of me and/or that handshake."

[2]When I brought this picture to the print shop for scanning, the clerk said, "Wow!" I told her, "Yeah, and the guy next to me is Ali." Her associate at the counter looked at it and said, "Hey, love the pants!"

To this day I cherish it.

After the Chicago shoot with
Cosell, the next was the following day
in Los Angeles, on the set of All in
the Family. Rehearsal and taping
started at noon and finished at dawn.
It turned out to be the longest shoot
in Family's history. The show wasn't
jelling. There were endless conferences
among Norman Lear, Carroll O'Connor,
Rob Reiner, and a bunch of writers.
Couldn't make the sucker work.

I amused myself by sweetening the
laugh track, guffawing on cue, along
with David Levine who was there laughing with me, and playing duets on the
piano and harmonizing with Jean Staple-
ton, whom I'm still in love with.

At five in the morning they got it
right, and struck the set. People were
walking away, bleary-eyed, going home.

"Uh, Mr. Lear," I said, "did you
forget we have a PSA to shoot? A commercial for the Democrats?"

"Oh, shit," he said, and called
O'Connor and Reiner back from where
they were exiting. "Come on back, we
got a spot to do."

O'Connor stepped right up to the
plate. "What are my lines?" he said.

Reiner wasn't having any part of it. "You realize what time it is?" he queried. "It's fucking dawn!" Until Norman took him aside, in private, and may have reminded him who was signing the paychecks.

THINGS GOT WORSE All the cameramen had gone home, and all the isos, the isolated cameras used to shoot the same scene simultaneously from different positions, had been shut down. We needed three different camera angles to do the spot right, and all we had was one camera.

As it turned out, Family's director—whose name I forget, but whose talent and heart I never will—could work a camera. Which he did. He lugged it from place to place, three times, shot the same scene three times, so we could do cutaways in post-production. And O'Connor and Reiner read their parts three times. Each take was within a beat of the 25 seconds of what I needed for the spot.

These guys are two of the best professionals I've ever worked with. Someday they will be famous.

Next day I worked with Freddie Prinze and Jack Albertson, Chico and the Man, and learned the power of vodka.

The script called for using as a prop the old van parked on the Chico set. Problem was, the van was parked, without an engine, at a different studio. One that Norman Lear didn't have access to.

I mentioned this problem to the propmaster where they shot Family, and could he help us?

"It'll cost you," he said.

"How much," I said.

"Two bottles."

Turns out his counterpart, the propmaster at the studio where the van was parked, was a Stoli fan. I had two quarts delivered to him at ten o'clock. The van was delivered to me at eleven. God bless Capitalism.

In all, we shot six spots in three days. I was so tired that I still don't remember if the Democrats won.

"Ray Teaches Him the Rope-a-Dope."
Ali and me in the Poconos, 1976.
Ali is the one on the right.

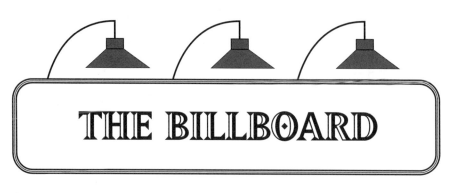

THE BILLBOARD

Sam Miller had just moved to Boston from New York, Y&R or someplace, to become Creative Director at the Bresnick agency, which was about the same size as Ingalls and a direct competitor of ours.

I'd met Sam at a regional awards show, where he was being supercilious. Sniffing at the quality of New England advertising. Compared with New York. Where they did *real* advertising. An attitude. Like a Yankees fan.

But I liked him anyway. Enough to be driving with him to Cape Cod with our wives one summer day, listening to him rant about the quality of Boston advertising, especially the billboards.

"What do you mean, especially the billboards?" I asked. I was kind of proud of Boston billboards.

"They're no good."

"There are some very good boards[1] around here," I said. "Especially when you get closer to Boston."

"They suck," Sam elaborated.

---

[1]And Steve Cosmopulos, a founder of Hill Holliday Connor Cosmopulos, designed about half of them. (He and partner Jay Hill did the "SKI ME" campaign for the State of Maine, and won every creative award for billboards in the country.)

So I said, "Listen, asshole, I'll bet you five dollars the next board we come to doesn't suck." Maybe we couldn't agree on what "good" might be, but we figured we'd both be able to tell "suck" if we saw it, and the bet was on.

So we start looking for billboards.

At the time there was a company called Bunny Bread. They were on TV a lot, with a goofy-looking rabbit in a cowboy outfit, and they had a jingle. I think the rabbit sang it. It went: "That's what ah said…Bunny Bread" [twang].

Strong mnemonic hook.

The Bunny Bread Company had just introduced a line extension, a line of buns. Hot dog, hamburger rolls. The rabbit sang about them, too.

So we come around a corner and there, half a mile down the road, is a billboard. A big 24-sheet paper board. And there, down in the right-hand corner, the logo starts coming into focus. And the headline starts enlarging from 2-point type at half a mile, up to 6-point at 300 yards, up to 18-point up close, and I wished it hadn't ever become readable.

Because there, over the logo of the happy rabbit, the headline shouted, "THAT'S WHAT AH SAID…BUNNY BUNS!"

Fucking rabbit cost me five bucks.

HARRY AND MITZY ON RT. 3 TO THE CAPE.

Design / DeNee Reiton Skipper
Illustration / George Hughes

KELLY

"HEY, HOW WOULD YOU LIKE TO MAKE A SMALL FORTUNE DOING THREE SPOTS FOR LARRY FLYNT?"

Kelly Naughton was smart enough to prove that the sun revolved around the Earth. He could convince you. Worse, he could convince himself.

He could also convince prospects and clients to spend as much money as it took to end up with a good creative product. I'd worked with him in the past on some political stuff, and he always managed to sell the good stuff and get us paid for it.

Therefore, Kelly was credible. Someone to take seriously when he called and said, "Hey, how would you like to make a small fortune doing three spots for Larry Flynt?"

Larry Flynt, publisher of *Hustler* Magazine.

What I said was, "How would you like to stick it where the sun don't shine," and I hung up. Knowing he'd call back.

When he did, he said this: "Listen, let me rephrase that. How would you like to make a small fortune doing three spots in support of the First Amendment." Shifting the emphasis a little.

Now, this I had to think about. The First Amendment is my Bible. When you write for a living, it has to be. I think Flynt is a pig, but you don't put him in jail just because he may be a pig. Pigs have a right to exist, roam freely. Just as rats do.

"Larry's being tried for the wrong thing," Kelly said. Flynt was on trial in Ohio for conspiracy, under the RICO statute, for distributing dirty books across state lines. Instead of for pornography. For publishing a cartoon of Lady Liberty performing fellatio or something. Right criminal, wrong crime.

"TV spots might affect the way the jury views the case," Kelly said. Fat chance, I thought. But I was a champion of the First Amendment.

And I needed the money.

So I said, "Here's the deal, Kelly. I'll write you three spots. On the condition that I don't have to mention Larry Flynt or *Hustler* Magazine by name, or even the court case at issue. Pure First Amendment."

Which was fine with Kelly, because the court had enjoined Flynt from mentioning any of the above. But sure, he could pay for spots in favor of the First Amendment.

Our theme was: Watch close, because the Bill of Rights is going on trial in Ohio. The spots were signed and paid for by "Ohioans for a Free Press." Not "Ohioans in Favor of Fellatio." And the spots turned out great.

My friend Carl Casselman directed the shoot. My favorite spot was a tight close-up of the Bill of Rights, so tight he needed a dioptor, essentially a magnifying glass for the camera lens, so you could see the blurred edges of the calligraphy on the Bill of Rights. And a Magic Marker came in and started editing out some of the freedoms we'd been guaranteed. Even the sound was tight close-up. When the marker came in, scratching out our rights, it went SKREEK.

"...because the Bill of Rights is going on trial in Cincinnati."

The copy said something like, "The way our founding fathers wrote it, the Constitution says we have the right to free speech and a free press. [SKREEK] But the way the State of Ohio *reads* it, if they don't like what you're saying they can put you in jail for 25 years. [SKREEK] So keep an eye on what's happening. Because the Bill of Rights is going on trial in Cincinnati."

Carl has an interesting voice. It cuts. Not an announcerish voice, but one you listen to. I wanted him to be the voiceover. He had hired me many times to be voice talent, and he was a tough taskmaster. Make you

nt of relig

se

the t

ssemble, and

hor a red

do the thing two dozen times before he'd let you out of the booth. So it was my turn. He did a read for time and level, which we actually recorded and used. But while the engineer was laying Take One onto the master track, I made Carl do 53 more takes, while I smoked cigarettes in the control room. With the mike turned off. Saying things like, "I don't know, Carl, could you try it again, this time with a little more energy. Maybe hit the prepositions a little harder?"

God, that was fun.

Anyway, a few years later I got another call from Kelly. This time about doing a print campaign for Chase Manhattan Bank. Having to do with abolishing every Cabinet post, de-fanging every agency from the Internal Revenue Service to OSHA. Jesus, I thought, what a concept. And Chase had the balls to get behind such a notion?

"...AND CHASE WANTS TO BE THE WHITE KNIGHT. TAKE CREDIT FOR TAKING DOWN HUMPTY DUMPTY."

"They sure do," said Kelly. "Somebody's got to start the ball rolling, all these regulations and bullshit the Feds are laying on us, and Chase wants to be the white knight. Take credit for taking down Humpty Dumpty."

He showed up at my office with, literally, ten pounds of paper. Ten pounds is the weight of one of those window sash things. So maybe it was more than that. Reams of paper documenting bureaucratic abuses from all kinds of government agencies, causing unnecessary pain to citizens. Make your blood boil. OSHA coming into a place with wood floors, a food processing company, saying, "You gotta replace this shit with tile, so germs don't grow," which costs a million dollars to do, and after the tile is down they say, "Hey, someone could slip on this stuff, fall down go boom, so you gotta replace it with wood."

That kind of stuff.

Kelly told me about a plane ride he'd had with Flynt, Kelly explaining how TV would help the cause. "We'll spin it like the cartoon is analogous to Jonathan Swift and Thomas Nast, the parodists, making a statement about the government."

"I like it," said Flynt. "Can we get those guys to go on television?"

I asked Kelly what he said to that. He said, "Not much. Larry carries a pistol."

Once, when an aide

disagreed with him about something, Flynt shot him in the leg. At least that's the story, and Kelly wasn't about to test it.

At any rate, I agreed, enthusiastically, to work on a campaign.

To do so, I needed a good art director. I wanted to make the stuff look editorial, not addy, so I called Rick Horton, a designer with a lot of experience in that kind of thing.

We spent days talking about concepts. Rick logged at least a hundred billable hours doing layouts.

What came out of it, to show how the campaign would look and sound, were fully comped newspaper ads, one of which I still have on my wall, framed, with a headline that says, "INFLATION? THE COST OF FREE SPEECH JUST WENT UP $1,203,000."

It told the story of a corporation in New York that had been hounded by the Internal Revenue Service to produce documents (every one ever written) to justify a business expense, and it cost the company a million and a half to do so. They won their case, but lost the money.

It was a beautiful ad.

And still poignant to look at.

Especially so because nobody ever saw it.

Because Kelly never had a contact at Chase Manhattan Bank. Never once had talked to a soul there. In his mind, surely; but never in person.

INFLATION?

On March 9, 1978, four oil companies and their advertising agencies got a letter from a Senate subcommittee.

It ordered them to hand over some information:

A copy of every single ad the companies ran during the past five years. A copy and a transcript of every single radio and television commercial, and the dates they ran. A record of every penny the companies spent in producing and placing the ads. A copy of every single letter, memo, report, survey, test, file, document or phone call to or from anyone in the world, concerning the ads, their audience, or their effect.

The companies' crime?

None.

The punishment?

Over a million dollars worth of man-hours to comply with the subcommittee's order.

Why?

You will never believe this, but it's true:

So the subcommittee can figure out which of four *other* government agencies to sic on the advertisers – The FTC, FCC, DOE, or IRS – each of which has the power to make the companies jump through the very same hoops *again!*

But there is some comic relief.

That incredible document from the subcommittee actually contains the following words: "Clearly [this] review by the Subcommittee ... can have no chilling effect ... on an advertiser who may be found ... to be exercising his First Amendment rights."

The Feds don't like what you're saying in your ads,

so they throw a subpoena at you with a million dollars of "compliance" tacked on, and that's not "chilling"?

You may ask why we're paying good American dollars to complain about problems that aren't even ours:

First, because we have this quaint notion that the First Amendment actually means what it says; that the "Government shall make no law abridging the freedom of speech or of the press." And any law, whether it's enacted by the Congress of the United States or by some jerkwater bureaucrat, can be equally abridging, equally "chilling."

Second, because we suspect that it's precisely this sort of regulatory rigmarole that's greatly contributing to inflation. (Ultimately, who do you think will be paying for that $1,203,000 in compliance?)

Therefore, we're going to put the First Amendment to the test:

Every week for the next year – or until they stop us – we're going to run ads about things that are none of our business, as a business, but which concern us deeply as participants in a free society.

Ads, in fact, like this one.

It has nothing to do with banking.

Mostly what it has to do with is the right, or maybe even the obligation, of people who work in America to speak up about the working of America. To raise awareness. To raise questions. And, when it seems like it's in the public interest, to raise a little hell.

Our Attorneys are standing by.

CHASE

Chase Manhattan Bank, One Chase Manhattan Plaza, New York, 10015

THE COST OF FREE SPEECH JUST WENT UP $1,203,000.

Ad designed by Rick Horton

At four o'clock on a Friday I got a call from Kelly's partner, David Levine. He said, "Kelly's in his office, with a gun, says he's going to blow his brains out. Door's locked. Wants to talk to you."

I grabbed a cab to Cambridge.

Talked with Kelly. He told me about how the Earth was the center of the universe, and how the sun revolved around it.

Until the cops came with a straitjacket and drove him away.

As for Rick Horton, he never charged me.

Art Direction / Tom Chandler

We were flying from Boston to Bermuda with a film crew to do a TV spot for Sonesta, a hotel chain with properties all over the world, and my partner Geoff Currier was stretched out in an aisle seat, nodding off, a few pages before the end of his thin book by some obscure author, when he had to get up and go to the bathroom.

"Let me have the book," said Brian Heller, a cameraman. I handed it to him. And he fished out a razor blade from his Coat of Many Pockets. If you needed a screwdriver, Brian would have one tucked away. Need a grommet? A light bulb? "What size?" How about a snathe, got one of those, Bri?

He takes the razor and slices off the last page. Surgically, at the spine. You'd never know it was cut. More to the point, Geoff never knew it was cut.

He comes back from the head, stretches his legs into the aisle, and resumes reading his book. His truncated book.

A few minutes later he nudges me, "Welch," he says, remembering my name. "Welch, you gotta read this. Strangest ending I've ever seen. Listen to this," he says, and he reads to me: "'Tanya unbuttoned her blouse, her nubile breasts only inches from his face, and slowly.'"

"And slowly what," I said.

"I don't know," said Geoff. "That's how he ended it."

"Strange ending," said Brian, from a few rows back. "Let me borrow it on the flight home."

Tyler Smith, me, and Geoff Currier in Bermuda, 1980. You can see the steel drums in the background.

Which gives you some idea of the kind of people I was travelling with.

When we got to Bermuda, all we needed was a steel drum band and a helicopter. That was Associate Producer Charlie Hoyt's job. The band was easy. Yellow Pages. "Need you to play Strauss' *Tales from the Vienna Woods*," Charlie said into the phone. "Two hours, hundred bucks a man." Done deal.

The helicopter was harder. None were allowed in Bermuda except for the ones that belonged to the Navy. I left our suite, knowing we'd be okay, when I heard Charlie saying, "So, what kind of rum do you drink, Admiral?"

Next day is the shoot. Tyler Smith is art directing it. We're headquartered out by the pool, me sitting in a director's chair under an umbrella, wearing sun-glasses, bathing suit, a stopwatch hanging around my neck, a crew of six manning cameras and reflectors, shooting the steel drum band playing *Tales from the Vienna Woods* on 55-gallon drums. Guys playing trash cans chopped and blocked into musical instruments. To this day, I think it's the best music track I've ever come up with.

A young woman in a bikini came over to my table carrying a pencil and a cocktail napkin. Looking at my sunglasses, my stopwatch. And said, "Are you...are you Paul Newman?"

"And who are you, my child," I asked.

"My name is Patti. Would you sign my napkin?"

"Of course." Noblesse oblige. And I wrote down how much Patti meant to me. On the cocktail napkin. And signed it "Paul."

Meantime, we're having a rain delay. The musicians have covered their 55-gallon drums with jackets and towels, and the film crew is all huddled under my umbrella, trying to get out of the downpour, ordering drinks and French fries and stuff. And there's Patti, under the next umbrella, with her girlfriends, watching us. With adoring eyes.

The rain stopped 15 minutes later, as it does in Bermuda. The rain stopped and the jackets and towels came off the trash cans, and the cameras cranked up and the helicopter circled and did its zoom shots as the band of black musicians belted out Strauss, and I shouted words like, "Action!"

We nailed the scene.

And I went back to the table under the umbrella to collect my cigarettes and then to help police the area, pick up trash, clean up after ourselves, and I gathered up some empty cans and candy wrappers. And a soggy napkin.

On which you could still read the word "Paul."

Who knows? Maybe if I'd worn bigger sunglasses.

Art Direction / Tyler Smith
Production / Terry Morris

CHARLEY

The first time I met Charley his legs were sticking out from under a sink. He had a wrench in his hand and a necktie on, sweat drenching his Brooks Brothers suit. "I'm Charley Sarkis," said the voice from under the sink. "Who are you?" I was the guy Sam Harris called, Sam being the boyhood buddy of my friend Harold Turin from Ingalls Advertising, and said, "Hey you ought to talk to Charley, because he's opening a restaurant and needs advertising." Sam might as well have continued, "And hey you're just starting out and you can't be too particular." In fact, Charley was not just opening a restaurant, he was closing one, forever: the old Boraschi's, a den with red flocked wallpaper and old men in suits sitting at large plates of linguini with clam sauce. One of their patrons, it was alleged, a long time ago, before my time, unwittingly accepted a bet on a horse race, and Charley was turning the new restaurant into a gentrification called J. C. Hillary's. So as not to be confused with Boraschi's, where old men in dark suits used to eat linguini with clam sauce and make book without even knowing they were doing so. And Charley wanted to communicate this fact. "I'm going to call it an urban tavern," said the voice from under the sink, where Charley was tightening something. Fine, I thought, why not just call it, "Not a mob hangout anymore." That'll bring in the lunch crowd. Turned out, what brought people in was a decent drink, good service, and middle-of-the-road American staples like hamburgers (for under $5.00), London broil, and beef stew. Nowhere on the menu did we say much about cholesterol. For that matter, we didn't talk much about anything on the menu. The steak and salad was called "Steak & Salad." No adjectives. Nothing on the menu was ever "tangy" or "mouthwatering" or even "fresh." We took the view that if it wasn't fresh we wouldn't serve it, and to point a finger to that simple courtesy would be doing a disservice to the place.

One of our early ads had a head-line that said: "We're All Out of Succulent." And went on to note the inverse correlation between the number of adjectives on a menu and the quality of the meals. For

Salad. If not garden vegetables, then what other kind? If not steer beef, then what other kind? Kangaroo? Blue jay? I inherited the name, J. C. Hillary's, and couldn't do much to change it. The sign was already up. But since Hillary was a fiction,

I could make him in any image and likeness I wished. So I made him in my own. Besides hating adjectives, Hillary hated puff-uppedness, putting on airs. His food could be called many things, including "stuff." It could never be called "cuisine." Which Hillary said was just smaller portions of the same item priced higher (he chuckled, with that

example, at what point in the following description, class, do we wish to bolt from the place: "tender, succulent steer beef served with farm-fresh garden vegetables in a zingy-zesty sauce." Vomiting as we flee from the Steak &

low-key humor he was famous for, handsome bastard that he was). For a logo, we stole an old photo from one of the Time-Life books about America at the turn of the century. Some dude in a group shot, maybe a bunch of college guys. Had a bowler on. Sideburns. So in our first ad, for the beef stew, he could get away with saying things like the following: "The Irish had a way with beef. My mother's way was to cook it in a great pot with potatoes and vegetables and let it simmer on the stove all day until everything turned gray and it all tasted like turnip. Mercifully, my father was one of London's great chefs before emigrating here in 1903; and as his first official act in this Land of Liberty, he gently told my mother "GET THE HELL OUT OF MY KITCHEN!" To me he said, "J.C., this is how you make the stuff." And the commercial goes on to tell how, if you don't let it sit all day on the stove, it won't necessarily all turn gray and taste like turnip, and you might actually like it. At the end of the spot, elated at this gastronomic epiphany, J.C. asks, "What on earth do you call it, Dad?" Dad answers, "Well, if it weren't for the sins against beef committed by your mother, I should call it Irish Stew." The word "against" pronounced with that snooty English "gain" in the middle. "I can't run that commercial," said Charley. "I'll get calls from a hundred pissed-off Irishmen in South Boston." "The Irish in Southie aren't your customers, Charley," I said. "What you'll get from the Irish in Back Bay is business. Kindred spirits. Who can take a joke." "I'm going to get phone calls. Bad phone calls." "Give them my number." And I got the phone calls. From the good ladies in Southie. Who invited me to perform anatomically difficult acts "Brace yourself, Ray!" would be how the foreplay went. "We lost four more today," I'd tell Charley. "From St. Michael's parish alone. They'll never drive down Broadway to East Berkeley and pay ten bucks to park and go eat at Hillary's. Ever again." He got it. Like he got that you don't need adjectives when the nouns, the meals, are right. In the many years I've known him, he's lived his life that way: "This is called Steak & Salad." Or the time I remember most vividly, "By God, you people are thugs." This was after he bought Wonderland Park, the greyhound track in Revere. He shut it down for over a month, and spent millions fixing it up, transforming it from a seedy racetrack to a place you could take a date or a friend, without shame, and for the price of a $2 bet.

On opening night, the fans packed the park and everyone felt good about the re-birth of Wonderland. Until an official from the Teamsters, the union that controlled the Tote-board workers, apprised Charley that he had a problem.

"We got some stuff in our contracts," he said, "got to be worked out."

"Fine," said Charley. "Let's work them out next week."

"How about we work them out before the first race."

"How about you stick it in your ear."

Ten minutes later Charley got on the P.A. system and said to 10,000 patrons, "Ladies and gentlemen, there will be no racing tonight. Or tomorrow night. Or until the track and the Teamsters can settle various differences. I regret and apologize for the inconvenience to you." My guess is that it cost a million dollars a day to keep the track closed–in the handle to Wonderland, prizes to the dog owners, income to the program printers, salaries to trainers, employee wages, restaurant receipts, etc. And me. And especially, the Teamsters. The track stayed closed for two months. Do the math. And don't play hardball with Charley.

Don't even think about it.

Art Direction / Don Manley

The All-Purpose Animal

My writer-producer friend Carl Casselman and I sat down and decided that advertisers were wasting their money on television commercials.

That was the day Carl had two wisdom teeth yanked by Dr. Kaplan, who gave him large doses of sodium pentathol with a codeine chaser, and Carl kept passing out onto the floor of the Fishermen's Market Restaurant between bites of the fried clams, which annoyed the lady next to us, so we drove to my place in Wellesley to keep from being pests.

I drove, with Carl slumped next to me in the front seat drinking a Black Russian he'd forgotten to leave behind at the Fishermen's Market Restaurant, and he said how being a film producer with no wisdom teeth was not what he expected to become when he was all grown up.[1]

On the trip home I told Carl about my idea for the All-Purpose Commercial.

I told him, "Look, custom-made TV commercials are all well and good for your big clients who can afford twenty and thirty grand a spot.[2] But what about your little guys? The guys with maybe a couple grand to spend? Most of them can't afford it. This offends my sense of fair play."

"Presumably you have a solution. A way to bring equity to life. Or you would not be constructing this elaborate preamble. Invoking 'fair play.'"

"Well, yes," I admitted. "It's called the All-Purpose Commercial, and it's built on my basic research into the All-Purpose Animal."

---

[1]This was written in '74, first published in *AdEast*, a now-defunct regional advertising trade paper. It's included here because I wanted to show off my skills as a serious thinker and a fine artist.
[2]Honest, that's what it used to cost. And that's with high production values.

"Does this derive from your deranged belief in the Basic Animal Form?"

Apparently I'd mentioned this to Carl before.

In case nobody has told you about the Basic Animal Form, I will set it down for you here.

I believe the Writer's eye sees things differently from, say, an art director's eye. The latter sees line and shadow unique to the thing that creates them. He sees differences even among the same species. Of animal, tree, house, person. So that you and I would look at something he'd drawn and say, "Jeez, that looks like Rover. Or Gloria."

To the Writer, however, all houses look the same. They have pointy roofs and four windows. All of them.

And all animals look the same. (Which I shall prove to you shortly.)

Once, when I worked with Milt Wuilleumier (Willy) at Ingalls Advertising, I handed him a storyboard I'd roughed out. "What do you think?" I asked him.

"That thing you've drawn," he said. "Is it supposed to be a cow or a horse?"

"That is a cat," I said.

"God," he said.

Which got me started on the Basic Animal Form.

If the writer, with his God-given gift for synthesizing, could enucleate the similarities among life forms, could conceive a shape, a form, that managed to combine the essence of Cow with the essence of Cat, then, aha! Were not other epiphanies possible?

Stripped of its trunk, was the elephant that much different from the rhinoceros stripped of its horn? Or the chicken stripped of its beak?

I was cranking.

It came to me that there was a general shape that differed from animal to animal only in the particular. The trunk, the horn, the hump, the wing. But in the general, the Form was stet. Universal.

Most great ideas are simple. And this, Willy assured me, was surely in the ballpark.

Fig. 1. The Basic Animal Form

My concept was to art what the paramecium was to Darwinism. The building block of life, from which all else was derivative. The Basic Animal Form, as synthesized by the Writer's eye. "I would be the first to grant," Willie said, "that you have a synthetic eye."

At any rate, here is the Basic Animal Form in action. To create…the All-Purpose Animal.

"I have always been a great admirer of your All-Purpose Animal," said Casselman, "and the Basic Animal Form from which it derives. In fact, I remember my astonishment at how much a leopard looked just like a rabbit, once you had proved it to me. I recall your erasing the ears and marking the bunny with little black dots, 'Voila,' you announced. 'The Leopard!' I considered it truly amazing."

Not many people notice such things.

"The very same synapses," I said to Carl, "led me to the All-Purpose Commercial."

*****

"I have in mind a 30-second spot," I said, "shot on 35mm, with holes in the audio and video for drop-ins. We lay in the specifics, as edits, in post-production. Like product shots. Product name. That stuff."

"I like it," said Carl. "Production costs get spread out. We syndicate it, sell it for cheap to a dozen different clients. It's a win–win."

"I have a script," I said.

Here is what I showed him:

AUDIO

ANNCR: Say, _____, when it comes to _____, here's news about a revolutionary new product that _____. You've probably wondered how so many other _____ in your neighborhood manage to _____. Well, listen to this! Independent tests have proved that _____ outperforms every other product in its field. That's why people are saying

MALE: I tried it. I liked it. You'll like it, too!

FEMALE: I'm enthused, and so is my family!

ANNCR: So next time you want _____, get yourself some _____. That's _____. Ask for it by name. You'll be glad you did!

Carl leaned back and drained the rest of his Black Russian and said, "You have done it again."

"Thank you," I said. "Surely you see the possibilities."

Fig. 2 The Dog

Fig. 3 The Cat

Fig. 4 The Rhinoceros

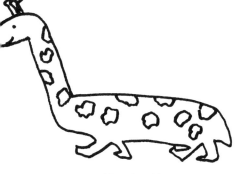

Fig. 5 The Giraffe

Fig. 6 The Camel

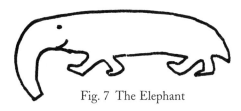

Fig. 7 The Elephant

Fig. 8 The Shark

Fig. 9 The Bird

Fig. 10 The Zebra

"Of course I do. But give me an example."

"Pick a product," I said. "Any product."

"A denture cleaner."

"Here goes," I said. "A little rough, maybe, but you'll get the idea."
And I said:

ANNCR: Say, PEOPLE WITH TEETH, when it comes to DENTURES, here's news about a revolutionary new product that GETS THEM CLEAN. You've probably wondered how so many other MATURE PEOPLE in your neighborhood manage to GET THEIR DENTURES TO SPARKLE. Well, listen to this! Independent tests have proved that BRIGHT ON outperforms every other product in its field. That's why people are saying

MALE: I tried it. I liked it. You'll like it, too!

FEMALE: I'm enthused, and so is my family!

ANNCR: So next time you want REALLY WHITE DENTURES, get yourself some BRIGHT ON. That's BRIGHT ON. Ask for it by name. You'll be glad you did!

Long pause. Then Carl said, "I can see it, I can see it. You want to do the voiceover?"

"I'd be right for it," I said.

"I can even see how it would work for multiple product lines. Client's got more than one thing to sell, but only enough cash for one spot. Maybe the guy sells motor oil and, um, toothpaste. And maybe wants to sponsor the Red Sox."

"Piece of cake," I said. And read him this:

ANNCR: Say, LADY SPORTS FANS, when it comes to GUMS AND GUMMED-UP ENGINES, here's news about a revolutionary new product that CLEANS YOUR ENGINE AND TASTES GOOD, TOO.

You may ask what all this has to do with Carl Casselman sitting in the front seat of the car on the Mass. Pike on the way to Wellesley spilling the ice from a Black Russian on his lap, with missing wisdom teeth.

Well, in fact the teeth weren't quite missing. They were in his shirt pocket.

We were slowing down for the Wellesley exit.

He said, "How about we give one of these to the man in the tollbooth."

I have trouble with this kind of question.

So at the booth I rolled down the window and placed a wisdom tooth in the palm of the toll collector. Who queried, "THE HELL I SUPPOSED TO WITH THIS?"

Before passing out again. Carl shouted, "PUT IT UNDER YOUR PILLOW."

Hey, tolls were only a quarter.

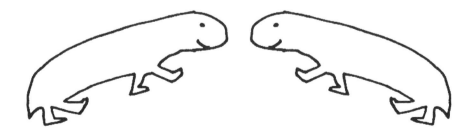

Design / DeNee Reiton Skipper
Art Direction / Milt Wuilleumier
Illustrations / Ray Welch

The All-Purpose Animal • 131

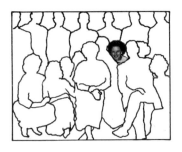

RUTH

I met my mother when I turned 40.

Actually I knew her for a couple of months after I was born, before I was put up for adoption. Sort of a "gray market" baby in which I wasn't sold, but was somehow trafficked to the home of some people across town named Raymond and Florence Welch who became my parents. They lived in the top floor of a three-story tenement on Ferry Street in the poor section of Lawrence, Massachusetts, which wasn't known for very many rich parts. I still remember some of it.

I remember climbing up on the kitchen table and eating a whole stick of margarine. I remember being knocked down many times a day by a black-

and-white mutt that my parents claimed loved me, that's why he kept knocking me down.

To this day I eat real butter. We own cats.

Anyway, they named me Raymond, junior, and the game was on.

When I was ten, Dad told me I was adopted. We were taking a long walk, as we often did. I burst into tears, I think, and I didn't get much sleep that night.

It was the only time I ever lost sleep about being adopted. They were my true parents. They raised me, loved me, cared for me when I was sick, fed me, put a roof over me, wanted the best for me. In the truest sense, Florence and Ray were my mom and dad. And if those aren't your real parents, then who the hell are?

Well, there's the genetic mother and father. The ones who conceived you and whose physical and mental proclivities you carry around. It may be baggage, but you're stuck with it.

So after Gail and I got married and started raising a family, my second, it crossed my mind to go hunt down my genetic parents and maybe get a fix on what might lie in wait. In my 30s I found I was an insulin-dependent diabetic, a condition that's almost 100% hereditary. Who knew what other buried landmines there were.

Coincidentally, at the same time, a friend of mine mailed me a column from *The Boston Globe* talking about a New York group called ALMA, a militant acronym for Adoptees Liberation Movement of America, sounding like it went around blowing things up. It was headed by a woman named Florence Fischer (a nom de plume) who wrote a book called *The Search for Anna Fischer*, about her quest to discover her genetic parents. Her battles in the courts, that lasted for years, and the "sealed record" laws that protect women's identities when they put their baby up for adoption. ALMA, I supposed, had some sort of literature they'd send you. I wrote her a note.

She never wrote back.

But six months later, in the afternoon, I got a phone call at the office. "Hello, Mr. Welch? This is

Florence Fischer. I'm in Boston doing the talk shows for my book. Would you care to have a drink at the Copley Plaza at, say, five o'clock?"

I would and I did.

Florence was about the size and shape of a fire hydrant, with one of the most beautiful faces I've ever seen. Radiant with energy. Jewish and righteous. I liked her and trusted her immediately.

We talked for two hours. She told me about her adventure, which took three years, in tracking her blood parents from a scrap of hearsay, to shards of evidence, to records in the Town Hall, to hiring lawyers to gain access to public records that were accessible to anyone in the world—except her. And finally meeting her genetic mother and father.

Whom she fell in love with and now visits weekly.

A fairy tale. A true one.

Tell you the truth, I don't know if my talk with Florence actually contributed to what I did next. But it sure didn't hurt.

I called the Bureau of Records in Boston, the archives in the bowels of City Hall where all the birth and death data of the past 200 years are entombed. A lady named Bridget Murphy answered the phone. With a brogue.

My adoptive grandparents are named Welch, Reardon, Donovan and McCarthy. So I know what a brogue is.

I spoke with her for several minutes, explaining that I wasn't about to blackmail anyone with the records, that I was starting a new family, that I had medical reasons for wanting the information, that I was a respectable businessman (you can look it up) in the Boston area, that I myself had a bit of Irish in me. I recited my grandparents' surnames.

"I'm sorry, Mr. Welch, I can't help you," said Ms. Murphy. "Them are sealed records, and you'll be needing a court order to have a look at them. People don't always succeed in getting them, you know?"

"All I need, Ms. Murphy, is a single page. The birth record for April 28, 1939."

"I'd lose me job for sure if I showed you."

"Sure an' they'd be the poorer for it," I said.

And then inspiration. I said, "Bridget, let me ask you." (We were on a first name basis now.) "Your brogue. That charmin' Irish accent I remember so well from when I was a tyke, is that Dublin I'd be hearing, or is it County Cork?"

Sweet Baby Jesus, have mercy on my lyin' soul.

I'd had one uncle who still had a brogue, and I have no idea where he was from. But I think over half the Irish who came over here in the 1930's came from either Dublin or Cork, so it was an odds-on shot in the dark at least.

"Why bless you, what an ear you have, Raymond! It's been 20 years now that I left the sod from Gilhenny" or Duncladdagh or some other damn place I've never heard of but it was somewhere near Dublin or in Cork.

There was a long pause. Then she said, "Ray, I take lunch between two and three o'clock. Me office is in the basement. Me desk is a gray one, the last on the right after the fire exit. Now, if you was to happen to walk past that desk, and a file folder should happen to fall to the floor, and you should pick it up and a photocopy of a page should happen to catch in your hand and you should bag it in your pocket…then maybe I wouldn't lose me job after all."

"Bridget?" I said. "Bless you."

That afternoon I had a Xerox record of every baby born in Boston on April 28, 1939.

There were only about twenty of us. Listed under column headings that said SURNAME, FIRST NAME, MOTHER'S NAME, FATHER'S NAME, DOCTOR'S NAME, PLACE OF RESIDENCE.

All the FATHER'S NAME boxes were filled in, except one. That was a clue. Another was that many of the names were ethnic, or could be taken as such. I look like a WASP, sorry to say. If you were cruel, you could even say I look like a Republican.

So I am probably not the baby in the first line under SURNAME, which is Fernandez. Nor am I likely to be George Washington Carver Brown.

I am most likely to be the blank.

The blank's mother's name is one Ruth Coyne, residence Lawrence.

Lawrence. Where I lived my first years. Click.

Under the column FIRST NAME is Ralph.

So I was born Ralph Coyne, by a mother named Ruth, in Lawrence, delivered by a doctor whose name no longer appears in the phone book.

I know because I went to the Boston Public Library and scoured all the phone books for Lawrence and its surrounding cities and towns: Lowell, Haverhill, Methuen and three or four others. I left the library with 200 names and numbers for people named Coyne.

Back at the office I started making calls. Again, going on the notion that diabetes is genetically transmitted, and that Ruth was more than likely a diabetic, I concocted the following fabrication:

"Hello, Mr. Coyne? This is Dr. Welch, associated with the Joslin Diabetes Institute, doing some follow-up research from many years ago. Is there anyone in your family named Ruth?"

"Nope," was the answer I got for the first 50 calls. I'd gone through the Lawrence phone book and into Methuen.

On the 51st call I got an adolescent girl who said, "Yes, but you'll have to take that up with Uncle Ralph."

Uncle Ralph. Ralph Coyne. The man I was named after.

"Is he there?"

"No, he's usually home from work about six."

"Thank you. I'll try him then."

At six I called again.

"Hello," I heard. The first word ever from a blood relative.

"This is Ray Welch," I said. "Doing some research. Any chance I could have ten minutes of your time, preferably in person, at a place of your choosing? Outside the house?"

"What are you selling?" he asked.

"Nothing."

"Then tell me your business right now or I'm going to hang up."

The voice I was hearing was blue-collar. Same as my dad's. And here I'd thought that my blood kin were at least nobility. I'd go take my rightful place on a throne somewhere in the British Isles.

But no. Uncle Ralph worked with his hands. Doing what, I don't know. But from his voice, he was not royalty.

"You might want to rethink that," I said. "What I've got to say is personal, potentially embar-rassing to someone, maybe someone in your family. I was thinking off-campus, where we could maybe talk in private."

"I got no secrets from my family. Whatever you got to say, say it now. I give you five seconds."

On the fourth tick I said, "You have a sister named Ruth. I have reason to believe she's my mother."

Small pause. "There's a bar off Route 93 in Methuen." He gave me the name. "Tomorrow at noon."

Tomorrow at noon he brought muscle with him. A nice enough man called (honest to God) Nick the Greek who was packing heat. I don't normally use terms like "muscle" or "packing heat," but it was that kind of scene, that kind of bar.

Ralph was skinny.

They both had folded dog-racing forms in their jacket pockets.

I looked for a resemblance between Ralph and me. Except for blue eyes, there wasn't any.

We sat in a booth in back and ordered drinks. "So you think my sister's your mother."

"Yes, sir." And I told him why.

"Maybe she is," said Ralph. "I heard she had a kid."

"You hear anything else?"

"No."

"How can I get in touch with her?"

"I won't tell you."

"Why not?"

"Look, Ray, and I don't even know if that's your name, I don't know you from a post hole. You could be who you say you are, or you could be a bad guy. Like in 'blackmail.' I love Ruthie and I won't put her in jeopardy."

I understood, and told him so.

We moved on to other things. Like what she's like, how he'd characterize her. *The Reader's Digest* version.

He poured the rest of his Budweiser and said, "She takes in stray dogs." So do I, figuratively.

"She's a gambler, bets on anything." I've played poker, a lot of it, for the past 40 years. "She chain smokes Pall Malls." I chain smoke Camels.

So much for tabula rasa and "nature vs. nurture."

"What do you know about my father?"

"Nothing."

Ralph told me he was one of six brothers and sisters, counting Ruth, all of whom were still alive, most of them still living in the area. Then the talk started petering out.

"Make you a deal," I said.

"What?"

"I'm going to write a letter to Ruth. Going to send it to you, unopened, inside another envelope. You read it. If you see anything that could hurt her, upset her, any potential to cause her pain, you send the letter back to me. Otherwise, send it to her."

He finished his beer and looked at me for a long time.

"You got a deal."

I mailed him the letter that night. It said, essentially, thanks for borning me. I turned out okay. Married to a great lady. You've got grandchildren. If ever you'd like to meet me or them, or talk by telephone, please let me know. I would be pleased and honored. And thanks again.

Three days later I got to my office around 9:30. The receptionist said I'd had two calls.

"Who from?"

"Both from someone named Ruth."

I looked at the pink "while you were out" slips. They had a phone number with a 213 area code. Hollywood, California.

I stared out my window for five minutes studying Newbury Street. It hadn't changed much in 20 years. Before I dialed. The phone was picked up on the first ring.

"Hello," my mother said. Her voice was a musical note I'd never heard before, but knew it when I heard it. A vocal resolution to *The Lost Chord.*

"Hello," I said, "this is Ray."

We talked, tentatively at first, then with re-solve. To deal with as much real stuff as possible be-fore the conversation stopped, because this could be the last time in our lives, maybe the only time, when we'd ever talk together.

"Who are you?" is not an easy one to an-swer over the phone. But we tried. For half an hour we tried. And what we found out made my soul sing.

My great friend Danny Carveth, blind since the *U.S.S. Yorktown* was kamakazied in the Coral Sea, once told me that the voice was far more im-portant than visual cues in reading someone's character. Sight is so powerful a sense that we're very aware of our own (and others') paralanguage: our smiles, shrugs, winks, nods, and sincere looks. We tend to overlook (if that's the proper word) sound. You can hear insincerity. You can hear honesty.

You can hear cruelty or gentleness. If you ever get the chance, listen to Harry Truman. Then listen to Bill Clinton.

What I heard from Ruth was intelligence, warmth, and character. Not education, charm and righteousness; but the voice of a lady that I thought I could learn to like a lot.

Turns out Danny was right. And so was I.

I invited Ruth to come visit. I'd send her the money or plane ticket. She had mentioned that wealth wasn't one of her burdens.

"No way," she said to my offer of money.

"Then how will you pay the plane fare?" I asked.

"I have my methods," she said.

Her method was to drive to Gardena and win $500 at the poker tables.

She was the first off the plane. Even though there was little physical resemblance, I knew who it was.

"Ruth," I shouted.

She ran to me and we hugged. We looked at each other closely, hugged, looked, and hugged. Like we hadn't seen each other in forty years.

She carried only one suitcase, which I lugged to the parking lot and threw into the trunk of my old Saab. I paid for the parking, pulled out onto the expressway and we headed west on the Mass. Pike toward the suburbs, an hour's ride. During which Ruth told me she lived with a woman friend, played small-stakes poker with some of the neighbors and cops and firemen and a sometime suitor named Al, who stopped by from time to time, and made bets with everyone on whatever football game was on television at the time. Odds meant nothing. She'd bet on the team on the left of the screen, you'd bet on the team on the right. Or dark jerseys vs. light jerseys. Or over-unders. Even up. None of your "point spread" crap.

On the way home I asked her who my father was.

"There are some chapters," she said, "that are best unread."

"Ruth, I'm the book. I'd like to know what's in it."

Many minutes went by. We drove from Weston through Wayland before she said anything. Then she said, "I don't know. I was raped."

"What?"

"I was in New York with my younger brother. We were staying at a nice hotel in Manhattan. There was a band. A man asked me to dance. I left my room key on the table. When I came back the key was gone. I thought nothing about it until midnight when we all were ready for bed. The front desk gave me another key. When I entered my room there was a man. He had a razor. He threw me down on the bed. When I struggled he cut me. There are scars on my neck and back. That's why I wear turtlenecks."

She was wearing a high-collar cotton sweater.

"Jesus," I said.

So Dad was a rapist.

"I'm sorry," I said. "I'm so very sorry."

"Don't be," said Ruth. "I have you. And you have a family."

Many more minutes went by. We were in Sudbury, a few miles from home.

She added, "And I have Shirley."

"Shirley?"

"My housemate. My soulmate."

"Jesus," I said.

So my mother is gay.

In an hour's drive you discover that your father is a rapist and your mother is a lesbian. Not your average commute from the airport. It makes you think.

I've looked into every corner of my mind to see if any of these proclivities abide there, and can find none at all. I suppose I could have been a lesbian, because that has to do with naked women, but I could never have been a rapist, and I can't even joke about it.

We pulled into the driveway at dusk and I introduced Gail to my mother. They were instant buddies.

A few days later Ruth and I drove to Methuen, to Uncle Ralph's house, to meet some of Ruth's brothers and sisters and their families. Not a great time, but not at all awkward. The whole cast of characters was interchangeable with my own adoptive family.

And that was that.

Ruth stayed with us for a week, then flew back to Hollywood.

A year later I made the flight to California and stayed a few nights with Ruth and Shirley, sleeping on the couch in their little tract house. Twice we went for the Early Bird Special at the Dew Drop Inn and had "ham with the bone in," one of Al's favorites.

Shirley wasn't much of a card player, but Al was okay. He held his own in five-card stud. In fact, he took me for $10. A couple of off-duty cops stopped by for a beer and introduced themselves. Ruth said, "Boys, this is my son Ray." Made me proud. Just as it did when Mom used to do the same thing.

One dawn a few years later I got a call from Shirley. "She's sick," she said. "In the hospital. Heart problems, diabetic complications."

I left at once.

When I got to Los Angeles I rented a car and sped at 90 miles per hour toward the hospital, down some superhighway where the average speed was 100. But I was speeding in fact in some other direction from the one I was aiming for. When a trooper pulled me over.

"You're in for a big fine, mister," he said, pulling out his ticket book.

"My mother is dying," I said.

"So what," he commiserated.

"I'm lost. I'm from Boston."

"The only answer that would save you," he said. He tore up the ticket and pointed me in the right direction for the hospital.

An hour later, when I got there Shirley was in the lobby with a friend, one of the cops. I ran in, sweaty, and said, "Sorry, I got lost."

She said, "We lost her, Ray. She passed away an hour ago."

"Can I see her? Would she want me to?"

"No. Neptune Society."

As a Neptune Society member you get to be cremated immediately, your ashes are thrown into the ocean, and nobody gets to see you dead.

We drove back to the house. Shirley poured me a scotch. Al and I played cards. I taught him a poker game I'm fond of called Natchez, a high-low Stud game in which a four-flush beats a pair and you get to replace a card after five cards have been dealt and then you declare, with chips, whether you're going high or low. It's an expensive game. It's also the most complicated poker game ever. I'm a master of it.

An hour later, my mother's smoke still rising to the Los Angeles sky, Al was down $200. He wrote me a check.

I tore it up and said, "In her memory. You watching, Ruth?"

Design / Marya Kraus Wintroub

Kevin White was Mayor of Boston.

"And Boston, as I've said, is a small town."

In Boston, what goes around comes around quicker than in a lot of other cities—certainly in advertising, and especially in politics. Mix the two, and the combination is swift and inexorable.

I'd gone up against Mayor White the year before, handling the advertising for Joe Timilty, who damn near won. Threw a scare into Kevin, who took the election by something like a point. No one had ever come that close.

The thing about Kevin is that he never forgets. Who his friends are. Or, on the other hand, who did the advertising for Joe Timilty.

But even though I backed Joe in that one, I was always a fan of Kevin, scoundrel though he might have been. (At the time of the election his office was the subject of more than one federal investigation.) So I was happy when I got the call about handling Question #1, a pet project of the Mayor's.

Kevin White

If it passed, Question #1 would allow the City to reclassify property valuations so that corporations could be taxed at a higher rate than homeowners. It was on the side of the angels and the little guy. Big business hated it.

I got the call from Jack Connors, head of Hill Holliday Connors Cosmopulos.

Jack would have handled the account himself, except that he'd been enjoined by *The Boston Globe*, a Hill Holliday client, from mucking around in any political campaigns or referendum issues, so as not to reflect any prejudice on *The Globe*. A law Jack cheerfully observed to the letter if not the spirit.

He was too much of a political junkie not to stick his nose into any campaign that caught his fancy. And too loyal not to help out his pal Kevin White, especially now, in his hour of need. Especially when the need had to do with advertising.

Because his agency couldn't officially touch the project, Jack called me. We were friends of many years' standing. Not so much socially, but certainly professionally. Shared many of the same views about advertising (outrageous) and politics (Democratic), shared information about how to make the agency business happier or more prosperous, shared the same black Irish sense of humor and loyalty.

Some years ago, when I'd just left Ingalls Advertising to go free-lance, Hill Holliday offered me a job. Creative director. Big bucks, small piece of the action. Gail could be part of the deal. What do you say?

Gail and I talked it over and decided we wanted to try it on our own, and the Hill Holliday thing was too much of a commitment until we'd tested our own wings, and we turned them down.

Flash-forward a few years, when Hill Holliday had made it big-time and moved into a couple of floors of the Hancock Tower, the I. M. Pei building that's maybe the prettiest skyscraper in Boston, and they had a three-day party, an open house, for *Jack Connors* clients, suppliers and friends. Everybody went. For the free *c. 1980* booze, to make a connection, or to pay respects.

"I went to pay respect. Singular."

Had a glass of wine with Jay Hill, bottled water with Steve Cosmopulos, then went over to Jack's office. He shut the door, walked over to his private liquor cabinet and said, "Let's break out the good stuff." Which he did, and filled two tumblers with Irish whisky.

He put his arm around my shoulder and walked me over to the giant glass wall overlooking the entire Back Bay and the Wealthy Western Suburbs. The view was spectacular. And with a twinkle in his eye that only one Irishman can recognize in another, he said, "Tell me Ray, *now* would you take a piece of the action?"

It was that kind of relationship. And still is.

When he sold the agency for, I don't know, $100 million, I called and congratulated him. I said, "Hey, I heard you sold your shop for many hundreds of dollars."

He said, "Boyo, I'll never have to worry about money again." And then he said, "Which means neither do you."

"Sure, it's bullshit. Or maybe not."

At any rate, Jack and I met off-campus for a drink and a talk about Question #1, the biggest referendum item on the ballot. The City of Boston had put up $1,000,000 to promote its passage. But the big-business interests had the money locked up in court until two weeks before the election. On the grounds that the City had no right to spend public funds on a ballot issue. The courts finally ruled that the City could indeed do so, and the money was sprung, sitting there waiting to be spent.

Problem was, there was only a week before Election Day to spend it. A problem most agencies would have welcomed. Except all the shops with any political experience, and/or decent creative staffs, were already booked, had their own major candidates or ballot questions, engaged in battle. There was nobody left. Except me.

Ray Welch
c. 1971

I had the experience, but no staff, save a receptionist who answered the phone for Geoff Currier and me, Geoff being another freelance writer who rented the office next door. And I had no media department to buy all the newspaper ads and TV and radio commercials, plus the billboards and the skywriter and God knows what else a million dollars could buy in a week... For Christ's sake, we only had three telephones.

I told this to Jack.

He said, "Don't worry. I can help."

The next day there were five more phones in our offices, each manned by a media buyer "on leave" from Hill Holliday, each one ready to buy as much newspaper space, or as many minutes, as every Boston newspaper or radio or TV station had in inventory. All three TV network affiliates, all the Talk and News radio

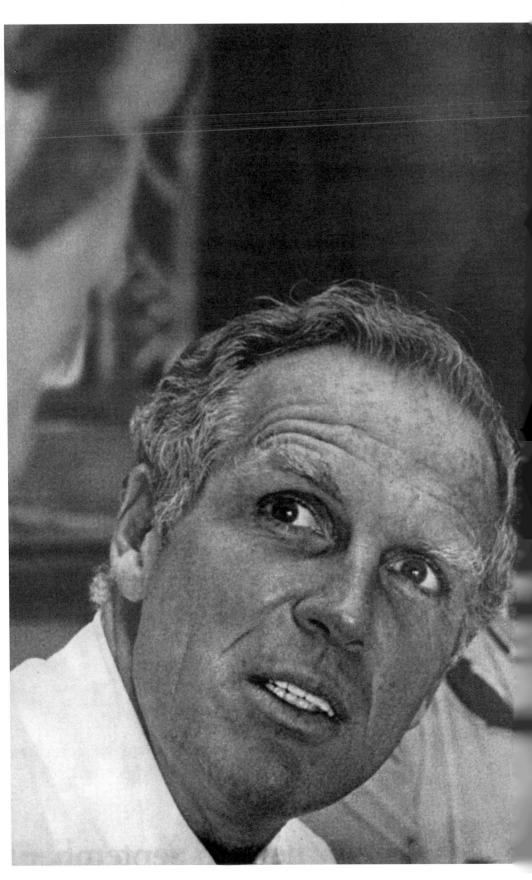

stations, *The Boston Globe, The Herald, The Hellenic Chronicle,* all the other ethnic papers.

I remember overhearing a call to Channel 4, the local NBC station. It went like this:

"Hi, how many avails you got between now and next Tuesday?" Pause. "Uh-huh, that many." Pause. "We'll take them."

A call to *The Chronicle:* "How many pages you got left for Monday?" Pause. "We'll take them."

Miraculously, we were able to spend a million dollars in a week.

Do you know what that amounts to, in terms of billings? Then I will tell you. A big national agency bills maybe $500 million a year. The biggest agency in the world, at the time, had capitalized annual billings of around $2 billion. And here's Welch Currier, not even a real agency yet, billing.... Well, let's do the math:

$1 million a week. Capitalized, that's $52 million a year. In Massachusetts only, which enjoys about 3.1 percent of the U.S. population, so multiply by 33 to get a ballpark. That comes out to $1,716,000,000. A billion point seven.

"Tell me, Mr. Welch, as president of the world's second-largest advertising agency, what do you have for staff?"

"We have three. But we're very fast. We do our own typing."

But I've left out the best part. The presentation. Where you show the client your ideas, show him headlines and layouts for the newspaper ads, storyboards for the TV, all of that.

I had enlisted Geoff Currier to help me with the creative, be my partner on the Question #1 project. He would later be my partner in our advertising agency. And Question #1 would have been one of the reasons.

Logan Airport planned to tear up
Boston. Mayor White tore up the plans.

Donnelly Adv.

When landlords raise rent,
Mayor White raises hell.

Donnelly Adv.

Boston loves a
dirty street fighter.

Be one. Help the Mayor keep the streets clean.

We worked 20-hour days. We slept in the office. We touched neither razor nor toothbrush. We were filthy. Until the day of the presentation, when we went home and shaved and put on our suits before driving back to Boston and picking up the ton of layouts and storyboards we'd done with the help of a team of "on-leave" art directors from Hill Holliday.

One ad listed all 351 cities and towns in Massachusetts, alphabetically, along with how much your property tax would go up on, say, a $100,000 house, if you didn't vote Yes on Question #1. It was impossible not to slide your finger down the list, look up your hometown, and find out how much extra it was going to cost you.

Even though we were down in the polls by two-to-one, with only a week to play, when I saw that layout I knew we were going to win.

"It wasn't just an ad, it was the truth, arranged alphabetically."

Outdoor billboards for Kevin White, Mayor of Boston

The meeting was at City Hall, the Mayor's office. There in the anteroom was Kevin himself along with his wife, plus Micho Spring the deputy Mayor, a bunch of flunkies, and Jack Connors hiding behind a drapery so as not to be seen. And Bill Matteson, a Hill Holliday account guy with slicked-back hair and an English suit, a Jack wannabe.

The mayor ignored us. He was busy with his people, City business. We weren't even there.

After 15 minutes he said, "Meeting. Advertising."

We all went into his office. Big, beautifully furnished, with a Gilbert Stuart portrait hanging on the wall as you entered.

There was no eye contact, no "Hi, how are ya." Just Kevin pacing around, making phone calls, talking to aides, anything to show he didn't know who the hell we were or why we were there.

So I figured what the hell, let's start putting these layouts where they can be seen; after all, we're going to have to present this

stuff, and I started displaying layouts wherever I could find a place to put them. On windowsills, chalk boards, backs of chairs, most of them on the floor.

Seldom do I present more than one or two campaign ideas; I'm usually confident enough in what I've done so that presenting "wallpaper" isn't my style. Home in on one idea, maybe two. But in this case, not having a whole lot of time to study the research, Geoff and I had come up with five different directions, each with a certain amount of justification, and we had about 75 boards to spread around. The office carpet was piled with Bainbridge Board.

The Mayor of Boston has yet to look at me.

Finally he turns around and nods to everyone except me. Geoff and I are sitting off to one side. Connors and Matteson are at the back of the pack, trying not to be noticed.

Kevin strides to the windowsill, grabs a layout, and observes, "This is shit." And scales the board across the room.

He goes to the sofa. And sweeps all four layouts onto the floor. "These are shit, too" he explains. "And so are these," he says as he picks up a couple of boards from the table and flings them as hard as he can.

One is heading right for the Gilbert Stuart. To destroy a price-less work of art. When Bill Matteson springs from wherever he was hiding and snatches it out of the air. On the fly. Playing outfield. Good athlete, Matteson.

Then Kevin walks to the center of the room and starts kicking the layouts on the floor.

"Whoever wrote this crap," he says, "is a fool." Meaning me. "This is the worst garbage I've ever seen. In my whole life." And he picks up and fires another layout against the wall, Matteson making a major league catch of it.

"He's insensitive. He's stupid. He's an asshole." Theme and variations.

By now we're down to half-a-dozen layouts remaining on the floor, un-kicked.

I looked over at Geoff. He was sweating. Seldom had his fine work been received thusly.

But I was starting to get it.

For one thing, there was no time to go back and come up with more ads. We were going to be on the air, in the papers, two days from now.

For another thing, (and this was the epiphany) I realized that this was payback time. Payback for the scare we threw into Kevin in the Timilty race. Payback for taking a picture of his home on Beacon Hill with the "No Parking Official Vehicles Only" signs in front while the rest of the Hill went begging for a place to park. Payback for reminding folks on TV about how the Feds had been snapping and drooling at City Hall.

Payback. In Boston politics, it was something one did. Like breathing. Or passing the hat.

Kevin stood there, hands on his hips, looking down at the remaining layouts on the rug.

*Art direction:
Dick Pantano
and
Stephanie
Westnedge*

"But as for *these* ads, these *few* ads," he said, "let's go with them."

He turned to me, with almost a smile, and said, "Let's go with them… Ray."

Question #1 carried the day by two-to-one.

And Kevin White knew how to bust a ball.

J. MARY CURRIER WAS A CHOCOLATE LAB, the color of our carpet at Welch Currier, and I stepped on her often. She'd see me coming. But instead of moving aside, she'd cower, shrink into herself, knowing the foot was coming, just blending more and more into the carpet, wincing. She was so stupid. Even for a Lab.

One day Geoff Currier, her master, my partner, drove to New Hampshire to sell his car, a classic (read "on its last legs") Mercedes. J. Mary sat by his side, smiling the demented smile that only Labradors can smile.

Long ago, I co-parented a black Lab who once wiped out a whole chicken coop, returning home with a mouthful of feathers. And a smile like that.

So Geoff drives up to the customer's house, pulls into the driveway, and has a cup of coffee with the guy. Chatting about the great tradition of Mercedes. As if Geoff knows any more about the car than it was brown and got seven miles to the gallon and swerved a lot.

They shake hands on a price, and walk out to the car to take a test drive. With J. Mary sitting tall in the shotgun seat.

Spitting out Styrofoam.

J. Mary had eaten the dashboard. The entire classic wood-grain dashboard. Little white shards of it drooling out of her mouth. Wet pieces of Styrofoam.

How she smiled. God bless her, how she smiled.

As it turned out, she was just practicing. Warming up for the big game. Which turned out to be against Carla Hastings, the ad manager of Cole-Haan.

Cole-Haan makes expensive leather shoes and handbags and stuff. They were Welch Currier's biggest account. Carla Hastings was Welch Currier's biggest pain in the ass. Some might have called her anal-retentive. (Although I swear, Carla, I never heard that in so many words.)

This condition wasn't helped any by the fact that Tyler Smith, our art director on the account, refused to do layouts. "I have them in my head," he explained. Meaning he had no idea in the world how the stuff would look until he saw the photography and started screwing with it.

Aside from that, he was a genius. One of the all-time great art directors in the field of fashion.

But Carla always wanted to see what the ads were going to look like before the photos were shot. "Who's the model?" she would ask. "How old is she? Where will she be standing? What's the background? What color dress will she be wearing?"

So Tyler would hold up a red dish or red telephone and say, "This color blue." And you could see Carla steaming.

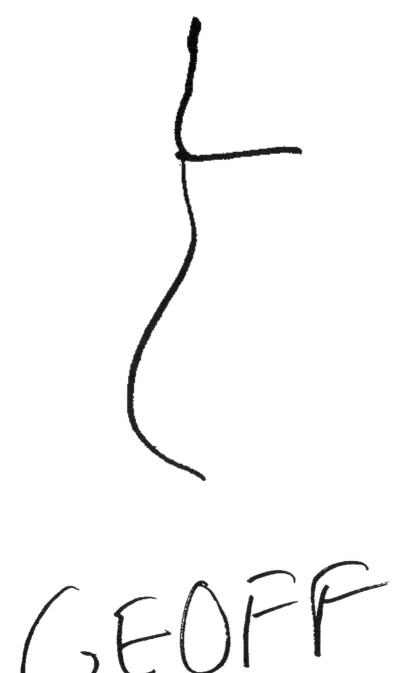

GEOFF

Karen Lynch drawing – tight portrait of Geoff Currier.

One day Carla comes to the office to go over the upcoming fall campaign. And Geoff says see you later, Ray, and he and Carla head out for lunch. Leaving J. Mary in the office. Along with Carla's handbag. This expensive Cole-Haan leather handbag.

I don't have to tell you what comes next, but I will anyway. J. Mary eats the handbag. And the wallet. And the credit cards and driver's license. And by the time Geoff and Carla come back to the shop, J. Mary is starting in on the eyeglasses. Smiling.

Next day Geoff gets a call from Carla.

He comes over to my office, gets a couple of coffee cups, opens the bottle of Johnnie Walker Red, fills up both cups, and puts his feet up next to mine on my oak desk. "Got some bad news for you, Welch," he says. "We lost Cole-Haan."

The income from Cole-Haan was about $300,000 a year. Losing it was not a good thing.

We looked at each other somberly. We clicked coffee cups. We sat in silence.

Until I said something like, "Hmfll," and tried not to spit out my scotch.

Silence.

Then Geoff went, "Snort."

And it grew and grew, from little suppressed snorts to giant peals of laughter, pounding down the hallways, your eyes watering, trying to catch your breath, trying to stop but you couldn't because every time you tried you'd just make it worse, and the next laugh would be a shriek even louder than the last one. Not since we were children, little boys, had either of us laughed that uncontrollably, pictures in our heads of J. Mary Currier with a handbag strap and chunks of an American Express card and drool hanging from her smiling mouth.

Everyone in the agency poured into my office.

"The hell's so funny?" someone said.

"We lost Cole-Haan," Geoff said.

And everyone in the room began laughing, the way Geoff and I had been, and it was maybe the best day in the history of Welch Currier.

Art Direction / Tyler Smith
Production / Terry Morris
Illustrations / Anthony Russo

V A L U E

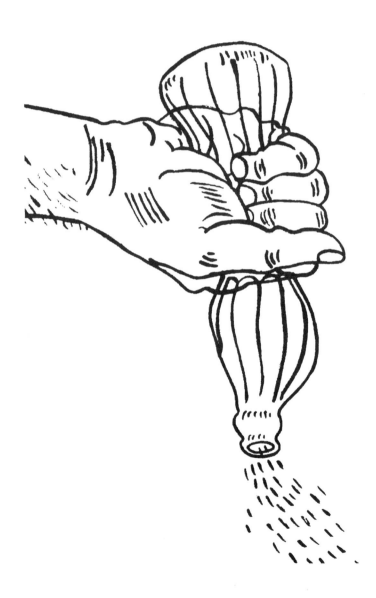

Threading my way back from the bar through
the crowd, I had my hands in the "I surrender"
position, a gin and tonic in each,
one for me, one for Geoff.

In front of me, agency owner Jim Mullen
was holding court with a coterie, gesturing with
his own gin and tonic. Our drinks met
in mid-air, and as we hunkered over shards
of glass, putting the little pieces
inside the bigger ones, Jim said,
"Hey, you guys making money?"

"I don't know," I said.

And I truly didn't. Welch Currier had been
in business for less than a year, and every month
or so Geoff Currier and I would look at the check-
book, leave something in there for overhead, and
split whatever was left.

Some months it was ten or twenty thousand;
others, ten or twenty dollars.

"What do you charge for an ad?"
Mullen asked me.

"I don't know. Depends."

"That's not an answer. My answer is $7,450
for copy and layout."

"Jesus, Jim, that's stupid."

"Why?"

"Well, a spread for the WSJ is one thing, and a quarter-page 'Compliments of a Friend' for the high school football program is another, and neither one should cost $7,450."

"I didn't ask you what *this* ad will cost. I asked you what *an* ad would cost. And $7,450 is the average price for each ad we produced last year."

"I still think that's stupid."

That was in 1980.

In 1998 Mullen sold his agency for, I don't know, something like $200 mil.

In 1989 Welch Currier went bankrupt.

I'm not saying we went under because we didn't charge $7,450 per ad. But I know we went under, among other reasons, because we didn't know the value of things.

What's a fair price for copy and layout? According to me, the answer was, "That depends." According to Jim, it was $7,450.

Who would you rather do business with.

Isn't $7,450 real cheap for a double truck in the Journal? Sure. And absurdly expensive for an itty-bitty ad in the local football program? Sure.

But it's a figure that does two things: It gives a direct answer to a direct question--even though you'll likely modify it in light of all sorts of variables like fee structure, hourly rates, media commissions, ramp-up effort, etc. But even more importantly, it speaks to how you value what you're selling.

If you sell your creative product cheap, you cheapen it. On the other hand, if you charge $500,000 for a logo, you're stealing. Either you're dealing with Coke or you're snorting it. (Therein lies another difference between ad agencies and design firms--a distinction we can talk about later, using words like "robber barons.")

So, how do you place a value on work?

How about hourly rates. Is $50 an hour cheap? Is $300 an hour expensive?

The answer is it's irrelevant.

If you were floating facedown in a river, drowning, would you feel good about paying the rescue team by the hour?

If it took Doyle Dane Bernbach two minutes or two months to come up with the Think Small campaign for Volkswagen, does that affect the value of the concept? Should a client pay more because it took you longer? Or pay less because the creative team got lucky quicker?

Only if the agency insists on time sheets. Which are good for measuring client profitability, but meaningless in measuring the value the agency provided the client. (And that's a whole other discussion.)

Time charges are useful, maybe even necessary, for things like account service, client meetings, and stuff that often puts the agency at the mercy of the client. Sort of like a taxi driver turning on the meter when the fare says, "Let's just drive around for awhile."

But making ads, that's different.

Every ad or commercial or brochure or POP or FSI or whatever should be assigned a value. Up front.

CLIENT: "We want to re-position our company."

AGENCY: "That's a big deal. It will cost you $50,000 to see our thinking."

Or:

CLIENT: "We need an ad for the United Fund."

AGENCY: "Fine. No charge."

Or something in the middle.

Pricing, as a reflection of value, is one of the hardest things for an agency or a client to grab hold of. Especially in the area of Creative.

Creatives usually feel under-paid. (As the story goes, "It's not the 20 cents I spent on the fuse, it's the 20 years I spent learning which one to replace.")

Clients usually feel over-charged. ("My cousin was an English major. She'd write this ad for $100.")

I don't have a solution.

But I have an opinion.

While we were still picking up pieces of glass, Jim Mullen said to me, "Listen, I want you to succeed. If you'd like me to come over to your shop and show you our traffic system, hourly rate structure, mark-up procedures, and how we bill things, I'll be happy to make the trip. To stay in this business, you need to gross 22%, and I'll show you how to make it so you and your clients both come out whole and well-served."

A month later, I called Jim and he came over to our walk-up offices on Clarendon Street. He brought dozens of documents, including forms and invoices, with clients' and suppliers' names redacted, to demonstrate how he did business and did so profitably and honestly. In Jim's eyes, Welch Currier wasn't just a competitor, we were a compatriot. An agency whose values--and survival--helped define the New England advertising community of the '80s.

Unfortunately, there were two of Jim's suggestions that we kind of blew off.

One was to get pre-payment of major out-of-pocket costs. Welch Currier went down because three clients left the agency holding a bag with about ~~half~~ a million dollars in it.

The other was devaluing our currency: the creative product. Why, hell, with all the profit we'd make in markups and media commissions and monthly fees, why scare the client with thousands of dollars in creative fees?

Why, indeed? Because Creative, at core, is the single most significant thing they're buying.

Not to diminish the roles of the suits, the account people and the bean-counters and back-office people who help keep an agency in business.

But it's only because of the Creatives that they're not selling a parity product. Good creative is the only true bargain in advertising. If you double the impact of an ad, you've effectively doubled your client's media budget.

The suits should not only be aware of that, but also be proud of it. Flaunt it. And charge for it.

In the early days of Hill Holliday, one of the founders, Steve Cosmopulos, when a client would ask him "What will this ad cost me?," would reply "$10,000."

"Does that include the photography?"

Sensing client weakness, Steve would say, "No."

"The typography?"

"No." "

"The mechanicals?"

"No."

Et cetera, until the client started to balk. Until finally, when the client said, "Does that include postage for the invoice?" and Steve would say, "But of course! Do you think we'd nickel-and-dime you?"

And you wonder why I've always admired Cosmopulos?

This chapter is all about pricing.

Thank God the rest of our business isn't.

But unless you get this banal subject behind you,
it's hard to go forward. Or you're going to keep on
walking into the same tree, and being pissed off and
surprised when your forehead hurts. Again.

And then, once you actually make a profit, how do
you split it up? Another tough question.

In the early days of Welch Currier, Geoff and I were
comfortable with 1/3 of the income going to the
hunter-gatherer, 1/3 going to client service, 1/3
going to Creative, and 1/3 going to agency overhead.

That's another reason we went under.

Art Direction / Don Manley

R. Manley by D. Manley, 1971

I met Don Manley a few years ago at a meeting of Rhode Island creative people. He was an art director. He was young enough to be my son. He reminded me of somebody.

I asked him if he were any kin to Bob Manley, partner and head design guy at an agency called Altman & Manley, whom I'd worked with on some projects in the eighties. A contemporary and competitor of Welch Currier, A&M was known for ads with breakthrough graphics. Cancer killed Manley way too soon.

"He was my father," Don said.

We toyed with the notion of working on something together. This book was the first thing that came along.

When he sent me the illustration of the Coke bottle for Value, I was rattled.

"There's an uncanny similarity in style between you and your father," I said. "I'd swear I was looking at Bob s work."

"That could be because I ripped off the Coke bottle from one of his larger illustrations."

"Good. 'Cause for a minute there it was getting scary."

We agreed that Bob probably wouldn't mind.

And anyway, who was going to sue?

in·ter (in tûr′), v.t., **–terred, –ter·ring. 1.** to deposit (a dead body) in a grave or tomb; bury. **2.** *Obs.* to put into the earth. [ME *entere(n)* < MF *enterr(er)* << L in– in–² + *terra* earth]

inter–, a prefix occurring in loan words from Latin, where it meant "between," "among," "in the midst of," "mutually," "reciprocally;" "together," "during". . .

miss¹ (mis), *v.t.* . . . **3.** to perceive the absence or loss of, often with regret or longing: *to miss a friend.* . . .

i·on (īən, ī′on), *n.* **1.** *Physics, Chem.* an electrically charged atom or group of atoms formed by the loss or gain of one or more electrons, . . .

Dictionary excerpts courtesy of Random House, Inc., from the Random House Dictionary of the English Language Unabridged Edition, 1981.

It was a small town,
and you looked out for your neighbors

We policed our own community, cheered for the good guys at the awards shows, partied together, hung out, had lunch, shared secrets and rejoiced in each other's company. Even though we worked for different advertising agencies.

This was the industry in the sixties to the eighties, a time so prosperous that if you stood on the corner of Dartmouth and Newbury Streets in Boston, and waved for a cab, dollar bills would fly into your hand and stick there.

That didn't hurt.

My roots are in Boston. A microcosm of the ad industry.

Boston was big enough to have all the talent you'd ever need—copywriters, art directors, photographers, production houses...but it was small enough so you knew who they were. By name. And if you didn't, all it took was one phone call.

Periodically we had dinner together at Locke-Ober, a venerable red-velvet restaurant downtown—a bunch of us agency principals, creatives, account guys—fierce competitors by day, close allies by cocktail time. Talked about questions that roamed all over the place: Who are the good people and who are the bums? Should you have a public relations department in your shop? How much do you have to pay to get a decent marketing person? All the way down to, "What do you guys charge for Photostats?"

As a result of which, for example, Welch Currier started a subsidiary that just made Photostats. Called it United Stats of America. Sophomoric name, but a profit center.

We were a mid-size agency, for Boston, billing under $50 million, known mostly (or maybe just by default) for our creative product. Our toughest competitors were the other mid-size shops with a good creative product.

They were also our best source of new business.

Terry Clarke, president of Clarke Goward Fitts, might get a call from a prospect, call it a bank, saying, "Hey, we're a $5 million account and we're looking for an agency; you want to talk?"

"Can't do it, already have a bank. But if you're looking for a shop, you ought to talk to Ray Welch. Or Jim Mullen. Or Tom Simons. Honorable people, good work, all that."

And my partner Geoff Currier and I would do the same for those guys. Whenever we got a call from a conflict, we'd recommend calling Clarke Goward, or Rizzo Simons, or Leonard Monahan, or Mullen, or Emerson Lane Fortuna, or Pearson & MacDonald, or Myers & Myers, or any of a dozen other different shops. All of whose principals we knew personally, and most of whom we'd either worked for or broken bread with.

NOT A ONE OF THEM IS STILL AROUND. Except for Mullen, which grew and got bought out big-time and Clarke Goward, of which Terry Clarke is the only one of the original bunch still with the shop.

Aside from that, gone. Along with most of the good times.

How come?

Fear.

By about 1987, the three underpinnings of the Boston advertising industry collapsed: high tech, real estate, and banking. Bam, bam, bam to the solar plexus. And when they went down, so did a lot of the agency business.

No more dollar bills flying into your hand.

People got scared.

No more sharing secrets. No more hanging out, making friends, having drinks with the other fighters in your weight class. All of a sudden, when you went to visit a rival shop, people would cover up their layout pads. Instead of shouting, "Hey, Ray, come over here, take a look at this!"

It was a sad time for Boston. It has been so for years.

A WHILE AGO I WENT TO THE MEMORIAL SERVICE FOR JAY HILL, one of the founders of Hill Holliday Connors Cosmopulos. I was there along with a hundred other people who shared, if not his life, his time.

At the service, I don't think anyone cried. At least I didn't hear anyone. But I know a lot of us smiled. Seeing each other in the chapel, going to the house afterward, swapping war stories, comfortable in each other's company.

The tears came on the ride home. Good tears. The kind that make you want to call up a former comrade and make a date to take a walk or have a drink or go hang out.

Jay should have died more often.

ERROR CLEARING

END OF INTERMISSION

Art Direction / Bruce McIntosh
Production / Ellen Adelson

The Voice *of* Tweeter

One day my partner Geoff Currier blew into my office with a script in his hand. "This any damn good?" he said.

I read it. It was for Tweeter, Etc., a chain of retail stores that mostly sold stereos.

After a minute I said, "It's very damn good."

Tweeter's schtick was to offer best-of-class components at various price points. So you could go to any of their stores and say, Hey, I've got $300 to spend for a stereo system, and they'd sell you the best matched components that $300 could buy. Same with $600. Or how much you want to spend.

They didn't carry all the brands— just the ones that counted, and could be hooked up neatly with other price-point stuff.

Geoff came up with a tagline:

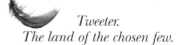

Tweeter.
The land of the chosen few.

Sandy Bloomberg owned Tweeter. He didn't see the deftness in the line. He said, "It makes Tweeter sound Jewish."

What the hell do you say to that. "So you got something against Jewish, Sandy? And besides, this is Jewish at the right price points."

No matter. Geoff had written this script, the prototype for hundreds of spots to follow if Sandy bought the campaign.

And I wanted to be the voice.

God, how I wanted to be the announcer. Wanted to lay back and say, "The land of the chosen few." With a wink in my voice.

The copy went something like this:

"So there you are in a listening room the size of a small Central American country, surrounded by high ends and low ends and no end in sight… So how do you put together a sound system that makes sense for your budget? Well, we've done the editing for you. Put together the best-sounding system you can buy for the money, no matter what the money…" Words to that effect. Ending with, "At Tweeter, the land of the chosen few."

Heady stuff.

So I said to Geoff, "I want to be the voice."

"Absolutely not," he equivocated. "Not in a million years."

"I'm right for it," I said. "I know how to read this."

"I know you do. But you're the most over-used voice in Boston. I can't drive home without hearing you try to sell me something. Clothes, furniture, race tracks…"

"I'm right for it."

"This morning I'm driving in, you're trying to sell me fucking muffins."

"It wasn't just muffins, it was a variety of tasty breakfasts you can get at Pewter Pot."

"They sell muffins, and you were hucking them on every station in Boston. Talk shows, oldies, news, sports…"

"Probably a heavy buy this week," I said. "Besides, you're my partner, for God's sake. You know my voice. You know that's me. Nobody else in the world is going to know that's me."

"Case closed," he said. "Stop pouting and help me think of who we should cast for this thing. I want to cast the talent and cut a couple of demos this afternoon."

Ever the professional, I suggested a litany of cliché voices, announcers who were as over-used in Boston as I was.

"You got a phone number for Mike McNally?" he said.

Mike's good. Character voices mostly. I used him for some Colombo Yogurt spots for which he did a great Peter Falk (Mike as Lieutenant Columbo). Yesterday I called him about another project.

"No," I said.

"Want to get it from information?"

"Sure," I said, sulkily, and dialed 411. "Yes, in South Boston, operator, do you have a listing for a Mike, Michael, McNally? One of those streets named after an initial?"

Pause. And what Geoff heard from my end of the call was:

"Yes, operator, you may have heard me on the radio."

Pause.

"Yes, operator, Milton's. That's right, the men's store. Yes, ha-ha, that would be me."

Pause.

"Yes, operator, Wonderland Park. That, too. Yup, that's me. Good ear you've got, miss. You into dog racing?"

Pause.

"Yes, operator, Pewter Pot. Yes, they have good muffins. Variety of other tasty breakfasts, too."

The woman had an eidetic ear. Ticked off two or three other advertisers I was the voice of before Geoff spit coffee all over my desk and almost choked. I thought to myself, God will get you for this, Currier. And you too, Telephone Bitch.

He left the office with McNally's phone number and a crapulous grin. (Is "crapophageous" a word?)

That was at one o'clock.

I spent the afternoon writing ads for somebody, I forget who, and at 5:30 poured myself a Johnnie Walker Red, ready to edit and exit. When the phone rang.

"Welch Currier," I said, all smiley.

"This is Geoff," Geoff said.

"Geoff who?"

"How you doing?" His voice had sort of a quaver in it.

"Something on your mind?"

"Well, twenty people showed up for the Tweeter session, and I tried my best to direct them, tone them down, get them to back off, but they still sound like announcers. All of them. So I figured if you weren't in the middle of something, you know, something important, anything at all, really, then maybe you'd want to come over the studio, lay down a take or two."

"Jeez, I dunno, Geoffrey. It's getting late, and I promised Gail I'd help make cocktails before dinner," I said sweetly.

"Damn it, Welch, GET YOUR ASS OVER HERE THIS MINUTE!"

It is a mitzvah, a blessing, being empathic. Being able to share another's pain. Weep another's tears. Cackle at another's anguish. So I went over, did a read, and got the part, which lasted six years, until Sandy Blumberg sold his stores for a gazillion dollars and they moved all their broadcast production from Boston to Florida. It was by far the longest-lasting and most profitable voice gig I've ever enjoyed.

When I joined Bay Pointe Country Club around ten years ago Rusty, the club pro, came over to where I was having a cigarette at the bar. He told me, "I thought I saw a pussycat."

"I'm sure you did," I assured him. Pussy cats being common around the golf course.

"Go ahead, say it," he said.

"Say what?"

"I thought I saw a pussycat."

"You on drugs, Rusty?"

"Say it! Say it!" he explained.

Someone had told him that Ray, the new member, was the voice of Tweeter. What Rusty *heard* was "the voice of *Tweety*," a cartoon canary, who does *not* say, "the land of the chosen few."

Just goes to show that even golf pros can sound like idiots. Imagine, some tough-looking bastard comes up to you and says in your face, "I thought I saw a pussycat." It is not the way to signal one's

intelligence to a stranger. Even to an ape.

The campaign went through several iterations, in which tag lines were changed and stuff like that. One of the lines Tweeter wrote (by its own self) was "Tweeter, for times like these." I thought it sucked, sounded addy, and refused to speak it. So they *sang* it. At the end of each spot. "Tweeter, for times like theeeeese." The Mormon Tabernacle Ad Choir.

Even so, it was a great run.

To this day, I'll hook up with a stranger on a golf course and after a few holes he'll say, "Uh, Ray, by any chance do you do… voiceovers?"

"From time to time," I'll say. A few holes later, usually during my backswing, he'll holler, "I know you, you're the Tweeter guy!"

And I tell him, "Hey, not a bad ear, man. It's been a few years now. Good memory."

What I really want to say is, "But not as good as this telephone operator I once knew."

But that would take some explaining. And we're out here to play golf, right?

The End

Design / John Pearson
Photography / Brian Urkevic

Sugar

Nearly every weekend, Gail and I play golf at Bay Pointe Country Club in Onset, Massachusetts, where we've been members for years, and everybody smokes. Except Gail.

It's an hour ride from here to Onset, which is part of Wareham, a blue-collar town on the edge of Cape Cod. And Bay Pointe, despite the pretentious "e", is a blue-collar club. Cops, firemen, bricklayers, Phys. Ed. teachers, barbers, and guys who put up drywall. Whatever that is.

After we play golf, Gail heads to a sub shop in town, where she and our housemates go for grilled pita sandwiches and maybe a white wine. Me, I go to the clubhouse for a beer and a cigarette. There's a lot of Bud sold there. And red meat. And there's a lot of smoke.

A few years ago, when I showed up solo at the club, I got paired with Dominic Conti, a crusty gentleman in his seventies, who crushes the ball like a 20-year-old. I have never seen Dominic without a cigar. Either clamped in his mouth or tossed on the fringe of the green while he putts out. We said hello, shook hands and shared a cart. I drove.

I turned to him with my sincere look and said, "Dom, would you mind not smoking?"

After teeing off on the first hole, he hopped into the cart and started firing up a cigar. I turned to him with my sincere look and said, "Dom, would you mind not smoking?"

He looked back at me Italianly, his lighter still torching the air. He stared at me for many seconds.

And without removing his stare he put the cigar back into his shirt pocket.

"Thank you, " I said, lighting a Camel. "That's considerate."

Dom didn't know me at the time. Didn't know what a wise-ass I could be.

But that was the beginning of a friendship—confined to the golf course, but friendship never the less—that's lasted for years. We don't know each other well. But we know each other enough.

There are lots of Doms at Bay Pointe. We like each other, bust each other's humps, and play a $2 nassau with the intensity that pros play for millions. Even though I'm a 20-plus handicap and most of the guys I play with are single digits or low teens. And after we play, we go to the clubhouse for a drink and a smoke.

So imagine our delight when all of a sudden there's a notice posted on the clubhouse door, Martin Luther-like, that says this is now a smoke-free establishment.

I said to Rusty, the golf pro behind the desk, "The hell is this crap?"

"It's true, Ray. Starting today. We get a hundred-dollar fine for the first offense, a deuce for the second, and then we lose our liquor license."

"Let me get this straight, Rusty," I said. "This is a private club, and the Town is telling us we can't smoke here?"

"Well, it's actually only semi-private," he said. "And as long as any of the public is allowed in, we can't allow smoking." On the course, Rusty had a cigar in his mouth as often as Dom did. "It's now the law here that you can't smoke anywhere that booze is sold."

"This is a private club, and the Town is telling us we can't smoke here?"

As in "any barroom." As in "at the bar at Bay Pointe."

Believe it or not, I'm all in favor of smoke-free areas, even whole smoke-free buildings like restaurants and offices. Nobody should be forced to breathe other people's smoke. Then again, nobody's forcing you to hang out at the Bay Pointe clubhouse. You want some fresh air? Then go outside.

The Town of Onset, it seems, had taken a cue from Cambridge, the most politically correct, self-righteous city in Massachusetts, maybe anywhere. Where smoking is felonious in any public place. Including the street.

You can sort of see where it came from in Cambridge. Home to MIT and Harvard and other places where they wear bow ties and help out the world by telling us, in the unctuous accent of academe, how to enrich and empower our lives. By not smoking, and such.

But in Onset? Where the average car is a rusted-out '89 Chevy? Where haute cuisine is the sub shop with the grilled pita sandwiches? Where half the people are Azoreans who won't have a cup of coffee without a cigarette? Where the centers of intellectual intercourse are the bingo parlor, the VFW post, and the Bay Pointe clubhouse? Give me a break.

"Good horse, dead horse, I say."

Now, the way most of us go about solving problems is a matter of conditioning. And early on, I was conditioned to manipulate the media.

Here is a flashback.

It's 1962 or so, and I'm a copywriter at Harold Cabot & Co., the WASP agency that handles Shawmut Bank, Boston Gas, and a bunch of other utilities. It is politically well connected, handling the advertising for lots of conservative politicians and referenda questions favoring big business. Sniff the air at Cabot and you say, "Smells Republican." I really do think Republicans smell different from real people. You never smell them on the subway.[1]

[1] My friend Gib Trub, a non-Democrat, says, "That's because we bathe."

Anyway, Cabot is hired by some right-wing PAC to promote a ballot question that would do away with Boston's Mounted Police Force. Save the City some money, they said. Cheaper to gas and garage a motorcycle than feed and stable a horse. And a week before the election, all of us copywriters are told to send letters to *The Boston Globe* urging citizens to Vote Yes on Question #7 (or whatever it was) and get rid of the funding for the Mounties' horses. Out with them.

Here is my letter:

To the Editor:

I do not like horses.

From my experience, horses are mean, malodorous animals that would just soon bite you as look at you. A horse bite hurts like hell. And can spread diseases.

There's nothing a horse does that a motorcycle doesn't do faster and cheaper. Let's hear it for motorcycles. They cost less to maintain, and leave less mess on the streets.

Good horse, dead horse, I say.

Sincerely,

Ray Welch

Next day I get a call from the *Globe*.

"This Mister Welch?"

"Yes it is."

"This is Charley Utley from the *Globe*?"

"What can I do for you, Charley."

"You the one wrote the horse letter?"

"Yes, I am."

"The one that says 'good horse, dead horse'?"

"Yes, sir, that one."

Long pause. "Okay, it will run in tomorrow's paper. I was just checking, see if you were a real person."

They published the letter. As a result of which I got hate mail. From old ladies in Cambridge who had never even seen a horse up close, so what the hell were they ragging on me for.

"I was just checking, to see if you were a real person."

Question #7 went down in flames, and to this day Boston maintains a Mounted Police Force.

But I had learned a new trick. To this day, despite being an old dog, I still trot it out. So I knew what honor called for. Even after the Beaumont Hotel incident, when Gail mentioned that if I ever again used the words "letter" and "editor" in the same sentence she'd divorce me. In a flash.

A man does what he has to do.

Here is the letter I wrote to the *Wareham Courier*:

To the Editor:

I am a diabetic. Sugar can kill me.

Yet, when I walk into many bars and restaurants in the area, what do I find? Sugar.

Bowls of it. Right there out in the open.

This is a heinous violation of Diabetics' Rights. We need a law.

Sugar should either be banned from all public places, including golf courses, or restricted to certain areas, like restrooms or parking lots. I stop by someplace for a meal, or a beer and a cigarette, and all of a sudden I'm put at risk. Little packets of sugar all over   the place.

Shame on you, you capitalist yellow dog restaurateurs and you spineless State Reps. It is time for legis- lation. Let's do for diabetics what we've done for smokers.

Take the fun out of life.

Sincerely,

Ray Welch

I put it in the mail yesterday.

We're kind of hanging around, waiting for the results.

As a freelancer, you have to make many delicate judgment calls on your tax returns about what is and what is not a legitimate business expense.

Or more exactly, under what column you're going to *put* this legitimate business expense.

I put my golf trip to New Orleans, Louisiana under New Business Development. I was there in NO, LA with Tom Mauro, my old roommate at Dartmouth, and Tom was in business, and you never knew where these things could lead. Maybe his business needs some radio.

Tom flew home before I did, and I spent a few days alone on Bourbon Street, where they offer you free samples of alcoholic beverages you've never heard of. Like Hurricanes, a nutritious taste treat made from moonshine and Jell-O.

After 86 free samples, I decided I didn't like Hurricanes. So I went back to my hotel and tried to remember how my day had gone.

I remember teaching the house jazz band at Café Bourbon to play *Men of Dartmouth*. I walked them through the changes, and showed them how to make "blue" notes. It is not easy with *Men of Dartmouth*. Especially on the "Give a rouse!" part.

There I discovered zydeco.

In the sense that Pasteur discovered bacteria.

As Calipho put it at the time: "Zydeco was born in the slime of the bayous and, if there is a God, it will die there. At worst, it will just stay dormant there, like a swamp-locked pocket of malaria. And not spread."

Calipho said that.

Calipho has no poetry in his soul.

For how can you not cry at words like these?

Oh, don' be mess wif de perloo,
Cuz de po-lice beez on patrol,
And de zydeco deacons be jammin',
An you mouf' gone come all swole.

204

This is from the soul if I ever heard it.

Not like "May your days be merry and bright/And may all your Christmases be white." That is not the language of the swamps. Where your mouf can come all swole. And all of a sudden at that, I bet.

I went to the Baked Stuffed Crawfish to drink Hurricanes and hear Creole music. Today it was Beau Cocteau and the Feelers.

Beau himself sang lead in the first song. In a tenor like a band saw blade chewing through a screw, he shared the pain of his (and humanity's) lost youth and innocence.

He sang in Cajun French, which you probably don't know; so I have set down the lyrics plainly in English. The title of the song is *"J'ai Ete au Zydeco."* This means "I Eat with Zydeco."

Here it is.

J'AI ETE AU ZYDECO
(I Eat with Zydeco)

> *I went all around the big*
> *   woods*
> *With my jug on my saddle*
> *   horn*
> *My little white horse all smash*
> *I didn't find nothing.*
>
> *Oh, yaie, give me some*
> *   snap beans,*
> *Oh, Mama, the snap beans*
> *   aren't salted.*
> *Oh, yaie, give me some*
> *   snap beans,*
> *Oh, Mama, the snap beans*
> *   aren't salted. [repeat]*

I have heard my share of haunting ballads, going back all the way to *"Shaboom."* None has brought me nearer to tears. Except maybe for this other song sung by one of the Feelers, a short man wearing an accordion. I felt it was sung to me and me alone.

Here it is.

COURTABLEAU
(Blue Courthouse)

> *Going out on the*
> *Courtableau,*
> *   dear,*
> *To gather kindling.*
> *Why, Baby?*
> *So as to boil crawfish.*

Going out on the
Courtableau,
  dear,
To gather kindling.
Why, Baby?
So as to boil alligators.

[repeat, with Frogs, Catfish, Fiddler
Crabs, Snakes]

At the place next door to Café
Bourbon I asked about the
lunch specials. Yesterday the
waitress had said "Frayed
Shramp." Today she said "Bold
Crawfish." The day's kindling
had apparently been gathered.

Calipho joined me at the table.
I bought him a julep. He rested
his crutch against the back of
the wicker chair. He sipped for
a minute before he said this:
"The lyrics are like the music.
They make the most out of
three chords."

As the Cajuns put it: "*Je veux
me marier,*" or "I look at myself
happier." Zydeco will do that
to you.

Tomorrow's lunch special at
the place next door to Café
Bourbon is "Bold Alligator."

But oh, yaie, I will be back
home in Bristol.

Design / John Pearson
Photography / Brian Urkevic

THE GIANT SNIFTER

*A*fter a hard day, I'd usually stop at my squash club, where I parked the car, and pour a scotch into a plastic cup for the 20-mile ride home.

I often made it a point to have hard days. The way W.C. Fields made it a point to keep a pint of whiskey handy in case he should see a snake. ("Which I also keep handy.")

One day I had a 4:30 recording session in Cambridge, at a studio I hadn't been to before called The Stable, owned by an engineer named Bill, whom I'd known for years. On the way there I stopped at the Club for the road scotch, which I used to tuck into the recess in the dashboard under the radio. This recess is the height of a plastic cup, and there's a slot just above it where you can shove the bill of a baseball cap, and let the hat hang down to cover the recess, thereby shielding the road scotch from the view of nosey passersby.

Saabs are good that way.

They ought to make more of that in their advertising.

Off I drove to Cambridge and, as usual, got lost. The studio is six blocks off Massachusetts Avenue, but you have to make turns, which always throws me. So I got there five minutes late and did my recording session, which lasted for an hour, said goodbye to Bill, and headed for home.

For me, going back the way you came is the only way you get back. And I was doing pretty well at it, coming right back to Mass. Ave. the way I'd come in, when I felt the tires hit the corduroy, the corrugation in the cement that lets you know you're doing something questionable. Like driving the wrong way down a one-way street.

Which is exactly what I was doing. And the cop at the corner of Mass. Ave. was there to help me.

"License and registration," he said.

Before I tell you what happened then, let me tell you what happened to the scotch. The road scotch, in the recess under the radio in the dash, waiting for me to enjoy it on the ride home. Waiting for an hour in the sun.

The Saab had turned into a giant snifter.

Who knew Johnnie Walker Red could be so aromatic?

The cop took one whiff and said, "Jesus! Get out of the car."

Which I did, fumbling for my license.

"Up against the wall," he said, patting me down for the pint he figured I had on my hip. Finding nothing on my hip, he called for backup.

Seconds later a car with flashing blue lights pulled up, blocking an entire lane of Mass. Ave., at the peak of traffic. And there's Ray, the successful advertising executive and well-known voice talent, arms spread against the window of a Chinese restaurant, with the Cambridge police going through my car looking for an open bottle. Or from the smell of things, an open barrel.

The cop who stopped me was in his fifties maybe. The two cops who responded to the backup call, looked like children. A man and a woman, apparently late teens.

The woman cop chewed gum. She said to me, snapping, "Looks like it's going to be a long, long night, Mr. Welsh."

Which by now I was having no argument with. While the man cop was going through the Saab, inch by inch, tossing things onto the curb. Like all my golf clothes. While the traffic on Mass. Ave. was backing up and people were blowing horns. It occurred to me to turn and wave.

Instead I was doing sobriety tests.

"I want you to shut your eyes, Mr. Walch, and touch the tip of your nose," the old cop said.

I did.

"Okay, now I want you to walk a straight line, Mr. Walsh, with one foot in front of the other, toe to heel."

Which I didn't. Couldn't.

I knew I had a degenerative condition, something called diabetic polyneuropathy, that attacks the nerves of the hands and feet. But I didn't know how far it had progressed. Had I known, I'd have told the police officer there was no way I could do the little trick he wanted me to do. Put one foot in front of the other, an inch at a time, and walk a straight line. Because with no feeling in your feet, that meant falling on your head. Or waving your arms like a tight-wire walker to keep from plunging onto the pavement.

Which is what I did. Not plunging to the pavement, but a lot of arm flapping.

"Oh my God," I said, only then realizing how bad the neural condition had become.

"You're under arrest, Mr. Welk," said the cop.

"YOU'RE OUT OF YOUR MIND!" I suggested.

Meantime, the teen-age male cop was still rooting around the Saab, still swearing to himself because he couldn't find the open vat of scotch. The sun was still doing its thing on the giant snifter. And the woman cop was reminding me of how much trouble I was in. And all that was running through my head was Kafka. "This is what he meant! He saw this coming!"

The traffic was now backed up for a mile on Mass. Ave., the busiest street in the People's Republic of Cambridge, and the horns were blowing and people were shaking their fists and giving the finger, and the old cop comes over and smells my breath.

"You willing to take a Breath-A-Lizer test, Mr. Weltsch?"

"Damn straight. Let's go."

He conferred with the teen-agers. The backup.

"Tell you what," he said. "You got anyone to drive you home? Take this car and drive you the hell out of town?"

"Yes, Officer. Bet your ass." At least a hundred people. Maybe a thousand.

I went inside the Chinese restaurant and called the studio. "Billy, this is Ray. I'm on Mass. Ave., in front of a Chinese restaurant, by the flashing blue lights. Need you and someone else to come here, drive me and the Saab back to the studio."

I told him not to drive the car too quick, though, because of a plastic cup in the recess of the dash under the radio. A feature they really ought to talk about more in the Saab ads.

Bill was there in five minutes, and in two cars we drove back to the parking lot of the studio. Where I've never polished off a road scotch quite so fast.

Art Direction / Jim Sinatra

Hitting the nail on the head is a
waste of time if you don't have a point.

In advertising, if you're doing your job, you treat the strategy statement like the Ten Commandments edited down to One.

Before I begin an assignment from someone, I insist that we agree to write down—and live by—what I call a Single Point Strategy. To help do so, I trot out my input document. I consider it one of the most creative pieces of copy I've ever written. This is the preamble:

Some weeks from now, after much work from all of us,
there will be a body of work on this table ready for evaluation.
At that point it will be untenable for anyone sitting in judgment
to be fuzzy about whether the work is on strategy. The following exercise,
while being a pain in the ass to complete, will minimize that risk
and help the project come in on target, on time, and on budget.

Strategy is far more important than execution. A lousy idea that's well crafted means you'll communicate your lousy idea with great impact. While a powerful idea, no matter how shabbily expressed, will at least gain you yardage. If you have to get rid of a warehouse full of mink coats, and your strategy is to tell folks, let's say, that the coats are real durable, then your grandchildren will inherit mink coats. Even if you had Shakespeare write the ad. But if you tell people, let's say, that they can save 50% on the things, you have a good chance of unloading the warehouse. Even if the head-line says "MINCK COATS 1/2 PRICE."

The Single Point Strategy is the chart. The ads are the boat. You can get where you want to go with a bad boat, but not with a bad map. Even if the map is printed on Kromekote in six colors and spot varnish.

I have a short fuse with creatives who consider them-selves "artists" and turn up their noses at "marketing" and "strategy."

They'll listen for hours to a prospect baring his soul, painfully listing his company's problems and opportunities. A million dollars can be made, a thousand jobs can be lost, depending on whether the strategy is right or wrong. And the agency or design firm will look wise and go back to the shop and huddle and wallpaper the conference room with layouts and logos and corporate identity programs, and a week later when the prospect and his people come in to find religion, the creative director will start the presentation with: "We have a great concept for you. We're thinking . . . we're talking about . . . *pink*."

Sweet Jesus spare me. "Pink" is not a concept; it's a color. And while the new pastel logotype may look fetching, it won't keep you warm in the winter.

My friend Steve Cosmopulos, whose blunt-object art direction and personality epitomized the early ads of Hill, Holliday, Connors, Cosmopulos, is fond of saying, "Helvetica is not a concept."*

Steve was so direct and on-strategy that his headlines were sometimes confused with puns. (Often because they were. But don't get him started on that.) In the '70s, his first billboard for the State of Maine's department of tourism launched one of the strongest campaigns ever in the category: "SKI ME." Which begat over 300 other in-your-face headlines including, "LOVER COME BACK TO ME." And years later, when HHCC finally lost the account, "THERE WILL NEVER BE ANOTHER ME."

Cosmopulos calls the campaign "participatory." The positioning was so obvious—"there's a lot to do in Maine"—and the execution was so simple that people who saw it thought they could do it, too. Thousands of readers sent "ME" lines to the State House, hoping to see their prose in print. Hundreds of stores, gas stations, restaurants, dentists and Roto-Rooter places put up signs and placed ads that played off the theme. A diner in Bangor had a sign in the

---

*And, "Make the layouts rough and the ideas fancy." And, "Making ads is like playing the piano; it looks easy until you try it." And. "You can dress up a corpse, but it's still dead."

window: "EAT ME." The copycat ads alone probably magnified the $125,000 advertising budget to something in the millions.

Around the same time, I wrote a campaign for WEEI-FM, a Boston CBS radio affiliate that played mellow "album" rock music, for which we coined the name "Softrock." Clark Smidt, the station's program director, knew what he wanted to say, if not how to say it. "We play a lot of Joni Mitchell, but not her hard stuff. We play The Eagles, but nothing raucous. It's not elevator music." He paused. "We just play the softer side of good artists."

He didn't know it at the time, but he had just spoken a Single Point Strategy. A good one. And the execution became a no-brainer:

> "Joni. Without the baloni."
> "The Eagles. Without the turkeys."
> "Roberta. Without the flack."
> "Cat Stevens. Without the dogs."

The ads were ubiquitous, and like the participatory "ME" campaign, our "without" campaign generated a ton of letters and postcards, along with ratings.

We ran a contest inviting people to try their hand at writing an ad. It showed thirty of the ads we'd already run, each of them only a few inches square, under a headline that said, "Okay, you think you can do any better?" It generated over 25,000 entries, more than any other contest ever run by a CBS station. Most of them were dogs and turkeys, but nearly everyone got it, and some of them were actually pretty good. An independent judging organization declared the winner to be, "Ronstadt. Without having to wonder which tune just blue bayou."

Another reason not to hire an independent judging organization to write your ads.

Anyway, we took our strategy statements seriously, often spending more time arguing about the marketing direction than the fine points of execution—the wisdom of the words, rather than their spelling.

The middle of the input document asks a dozen necessary, predictable questions about the target audience, its demographics and psychographics, the state of the marketplace, media, budgets, unique opportunities, sacred cows, deadlines and review dates. But the first and last questions are fiendish, and can win or lose the business on their own hook.

———————————

I read the preamble aloud to the client people: "*Some weeks from now, after much work from all of us, there will be a body of work on this table…*" Sounds reasonable. Ought to take us two minutes, right? Let's get on with it.

Okay, then, let's just tear through item number-one here. Item number-one is a simple question, no big words, just as the rest of the items are. Oh so simple:

"Why are we doing this project in the first place?"

At the table are the VP/marketing, the VP/sales, the advertising director, the ad manager and her assistant, somebody from operations or manufacturing or engineering, and somebody who looks like he got on the wrong bus.

They all look at me funny. "What do you mean, 'Why are we doing this project in the first place?'"

"I mean, why do you want me to make these ads for you?"

"To sell our product."

"Ed, you guys make infrared components that sell for a $100,000 a pop to an audience of 250 companies in the entire world. You think someone with purchasing power in that universe is going to look at an ad, pick up the phone and order one of your gizmos?"

"No, of course not."

"Then maybe you'd agree that we aren't making ads in order to sell things?"

"Well then, if the ads aren't going to sell, why are we advertising in the first place?"

"That's sort of what my question is about, Ed. Why are we sitting here talking about doing ads if the ads aren't supposed to sell anything?"

"Well, at least we want to get inquiries."

"From whom in the target audience to whom here?"

"From the purchasing department there to Charley here. Charley in sales."

Susan interrupts. "No, that's not always right, Ed. Usually the call comes from one of their system designers who needs information from Pete in engineering. Then the systems guy kicks it over to manufacturing, and it doesn't get to purchasing until someone in operations signs off on it. With a lot of customers, anything over $10,000 has to go that route."

"Then who are we talking to?" I ask. "The systems designer or his boss?"

"The system designer," says Pete.

"The boss," says Margaret.

"Both of them," says Kurt, the VP/Marketing, whose last job was with Procter & Gamble. "I think we ought to be in horizontal business books like *Fortune*, where we reach the top people, generate some downward push. Call me silly, but I can even see us on television, like on *Meet the Press* or *Letterman*. That way you reach every decision-maker at every level, and create top-of-mind awareness among the heat-seekers and early adopters in the target and a comfort level enterprise-wide," prancing out his shiniest marketing-jargon ponies.

Okay, I say to myself, I'll call you silly; *Meet the Press* doesn't take commercials, and *Letterman* doesn't take promissory notes on next year's advertising budget.

"Can we afford to go on TV, Ray?"

"No," I say.

"But Petco was on TV. Remember them? With a hand puppet? We're as big as Petco. We could do something like that, couldn't we?"

"No," I say. "The price of hand puppets is out of sight."

So far, nobody has come within six feet of a smart answer to why they want me to make ads for them. And we haven't even got to the next simple question, which is:

Within reason, what action can we expect from the people we're talking to?

Which often elicits answers like "Email us for more information."

"Okay," I say. "Who should get the email?"

"Charley in sales."

"Pete in engineering."

And they're chasing each other's tails again.

At the end of the meeting I advise them to hire two more salespeople and not waste a nickel on advertising.

―――――――――

The final question on my little quiz is sadistic. Whatever part of my brain devised it, I'm ashamed of it; it will land me in Hell.

In one sentence without commas, conjunctions or words like "best,"
please complete the following statement:
The single most important thing we must communicate is _____

I'm at an input meeting with five executives from a chain of men's stores. We're on the final question. I say to Jennifer the advertising manager, "You want to start off?"

"Sure," she says. "We sell the highest quality menswear at the lowest possible price."

I won't quibble about "highest quality" being a weasel-word substitute for the verboten "best." But she has trod on the cardinal rule: no conjunctions. "Single Point," remember? And even though "at" is usually a preposition, the way she's using it here smells a lot like a conjunction to me, and I'm not about to lead the client into a strategy that's trying to send the boat in two directions at once. Boats don't like to sail that way. "Uh, which is it, Jennifer, 'best quality' or 'lowest price'?"

"Well, it's both."

"You can't have both," I say. In the tone of voice of "Thou shall not commit a two-headed strategy."

In his workshop, Cosmopulos once built, and still carries around with him to presentations, a bed of nails. It takes no magic to lie down on such a thing, the many nail points, no matter how sharp, each bearing very few pounds-per-square-inch of weight. He invites prospects to push their hands down on it. Which they do, gingerly at first, but then curiously and firmly. Amazed that they're not pin-cushioned. Then Cosmo removes a section of the bed with only a single nail sticking up in the air. He invites the prospects to press down on it now.

They get it. They don't even try.

"They're both wrong anyway," says Gerard the buyer. "The reason people shop here is the designer brands. So my answer is, 'We're the only store that offers Calvin Klein and St. Laurent and Joseph Aboud and HSM and Tommy under the same roof, all at discounted prices, with salespeople who know what they're doing. Simple as that."

It trips off the tongue like a drunk falling downstairs.

"Where's that coming from, Gerard?" says Morris, the founder. "You don't think it's the six convenient locations that keep us in business? We've got to tell people we've got six convenient locations. And we should list them all. All the addresses. In every ad. I'm telling you right now I won't approve a single ad that doesn't mention all six convenient locations. Including the new one in Swansea that opens in September."

"That's crazy, Morris," someone says. "TV spots are only thirty seconds long. We can't spend twenty of them listing store locations!"

"Then just say 'Six convenient locations near you. Close to where you live or work.' I can live with that. Plus free tailoring."

Someone thinks we should be selling the security of a wardrobe selected for you by a salesman who knows what colors go with what. Someone else thinks we should emphasize that we're young and hip. Not just an old man's store anymore.

Morris shuts his eyes.

So do I. I listen. I hear six people who have known each other for years arguing passionately about what they collectively do for a living and what's their reason for existence, and what value do they add to the world. I close my eyes and see storm-battered boats without charts or rudders, trying to make headway sideways, with the captain yelling "Hard a-port!" And the helmsman wheeling furiously to starboard. Pretty soon they're going to sink, and even though they'll never admit it aloud, everybody knows it.

And then Mel the sales manager hits the nail on the head: "Here to serve your every designer clothing need," he says, proud of himself for not using a conjunction.

But Mel has just used a phrase you've seen, with only the subject changed six-thousand times. It is meaningless: "Serving all your _____ needs."

"Serving all your banking needs." "Here to serve your every plumbing need." "We serve all your cheese needs." A bottled-water distributor in Rhode Island boasts, "Serving your every hydration need." I forget what they were selling, but I swear to God there's an outfit in Boston whose positioning line is the stripped-down no-frills, "Here to serve your every need." That's all folks!

And is designer clothing a "need" in the first place? Sex and food and cigarettes, I guess, are "needs." But designer clothing? Give me a break. The plural noun "needs," other than when you apply it to primal cravings, is a word not heard in nature. It's an off-key construct of bad ad makers.

As is "When it comes to . . ."

Dan Reeves, a creative director pal of mine, collects tear sheets of ads that start off, "When it comes to . . ." As in, "When it comes to fertilizer, Scotts is here to serve your every lawn care need." The "from . . . to" twins pop up a lot as well. As in, "From paint to plaster, from rugs to roofing, we can serve your every home improvement need."

At any rate, we took our strategy statements seriously. Partly because they're necessary navigational tools; and partly because, at the end of hammering them out with the client, we'd all end up on the same side. No more "us *vs.* them," the crazy creatives *vs.* the people who *really* know the business.

To a copywriter, "You make it sound easy" is high praise. And strategy statements, just like copy, ought to sound easy.

Most marketing people I've met, on both the agency and client side, make it sound hard. They think in ad-speak and talk in jargon. Instead of "Stop by your Ford dealer," they prefer "Visit your local participating authorized Ford dealer today." On the grounds that "local" means "convenient," right? And it's only the "participating" Ford dealers who are paying for this ad, right? And we wouldn't want a consumer falling into the hands of none of those *un*-authorized dealers, the ones selling all those counterfeit Fords, would we? And of course we have to say "today" otherwise one might wait until tomorrow or some other damn day, right? If you'd majored in Marketing instead of English you'd know that.

What I know is that most marketing people can't write two sentences in a row without jargon or without underestimating the consumer. Make that one sentence in a row. And I know that Geoff Currier and I and a few other creatives gave clients more solid marketing advice than did any dozen marketing people whose education stopped in business school.

Some of our accounts, the smart ones, knew all about

that. They followed our advice, no matter how risky it may have looked on the surface, and they prospered for doing so.

Michael Shane had been a client of mine since the 1970s, when I worked on one of his first ventures, a fashion jeans company that I named Faded Glory. In the early '80s, he started a computer company called Leading Edge, which private-labeled IBM computer rip-offs. Michael was known as the Clone King, at one time being the third-largest PC brand in the country. From computers he branched into printers and monitors and such, which he sold alongside the OEM-branded peripherals, for about one-third less than the manufacturers' products.

After that, on the notion that there's more profit in selling the blades than the razors, he decided to sell his own line of floppy disks. He asked me to create a name for the brand. I came up with Elephant.

Elephant. "Never forgets."

Rollin Binzer designed a West Coast logo of a mythic, metallic high-tech pachyderm staring at you, a gleam in his third eye, knowing more than he let on. In bright orange-and-yellow-and-black packages that contrasted stridently with IBM's safe, sedate silver-and-blue. Similarly garish ads jumped off the pages of the trade books.

Elephant was conceived as a price-point item, a discount disk. Instead, because of the outrageous-looking ads and packaging—not to mention the strange name—it became a premium product, the highest-margin floppy on the market and the best-selling diskette in history.

When I presented the Elephant concept to Leading Edge, we went around the conference table taking votes. Besides Michael, there were five other Leading Edge executives present: brand managers, product managers, VP/Sales, VP/Marketing, etc.

With only one exception, they hated what they saw.

"Elephants are big and bulky. I don't think that's what we want to convey."

"Magnetic media integrity is serious stuff to the end-user. It doesn't look serious enough."

"I think of 'white' elephants. Obsolete."

One guy actually said, "Elephants are dinosaurs."

And so on around the table. Until the buck got passed around to Michael, who said, "I love it" and went on to make millions with the brand. Democracy in action is a wonderful thing to behold.

Here was a me-too item, a parity product (except for the packaging) that dominated the category for a few years until Michael sold the brand to Dennison—the very company that manufactured the disks for Elephant—whose marketing people promptly ran the brand into the ground. They never got it that they weren't selling a parity product, they were selling a cult item, a brand that flew in the face of nerdism the way Dilbert does.

But Michael Shane got it. As he did with a lot of other things. He knew that implicit in the name and the look there was a Single Point Strategy: "Reduce the choices down to two." Make the choice either Elephant or "all others."

Murray Pearlstein is another client who got it. Murray owns a men's store in Boston called Louis. I think it's the priciest men's store in the world.

One day he asked Geoff for an ad that addressed why a suit from Louis cost so damn much money. Geoff's headline was: "Why a suit from Louis costs so damn much money."

I remember some marketing lady from another shop saying at the time, "That's stupid, it's an admission that your clothes are expensive."

Right. And then the ad took the problematic (and accurate) perception of high price and held it up by the neck and throttled it to death. Louis is still around, more expensive and profitable than ever.

———————

Way beyond advertising and marketing, Single Point Strategies have enormous power. Good ones can lead to the betterment of Man; bad ones can (and do) kill.

My favorite good one is this: *Do unto others as you'd have them do unto you.*

To know how to live, it's all you need to know.

You don't need the Bible or the Koran. At best, all they do is amplify the concept. At worst, meaning most of the time, they muck it up with rules and regs and ambiguous agendas. Most of which, in the name of interpretation, just muddy the most elegant policy ever set down.

Good strategy doesn't need "interpretation." It speaks plain, and it speaks to everyone.

Unfocused strategy leads to bad policy. As policy, the Ten Commandments are pretty slovenly wrought. Some of them aren't too bad conceptually, but there are way too many of them. Like the tax laws.

"Thou shall not kill" is at least pretty clear and to the point (not that it deters Texas from capital punishment), but it deserves a bigger type size than the rest of them. As far as Commandments go, it's the ace of trumps.

If you steal too much from me, or covet my wife too loudly, then I'll kill you. That may signify a bad attitude on my part, but it tends to chill the practice of other evils on the laundry list.

But the one about placing "no false gods before Me"? That cowflap of a Commandment has probably launched more human misery, more jihads and inquisitions and missionary meddling, than anything else ever written. Even by people like Hitler.

Ironically—no, make that fittingly—it's the single Commandment that isn't subsumed by the simple "Do unto others . . ."

The only one.

Can you conceive of any other policy that could cause so much mischief? And what does it tell you about Single Point Strategy.

If our priests and pols would just put away all their Holy Books and shake hands on the Golden Rule, we would have us a far finer world.

Here's another strategy I like: *All men are created equal.* By God, you could start a government with that one.

Copywriter Mark Myers's uncle was a dentist. He once asked Mark why good advertising was so hard to write. Mark thought for a minute before answering.

"Let's say I come to you for a set of false teeth. You say sure, and make imprints and take x-rays of my mouth and so forth, and you tell me to come back in two weeks. So I come back and my new teeth are ready. You hand me the mirror and I look into it and smile at myself.

"You say, 'Well, then! What do you think, Mark?'"

"And I frown and say, 'Frankly, Uncle, I'm a little disappointed. For one thing, they're white. *Everyone's* got white teeth. They don't stand out. Can't we make them red? Or how about something in a plaid? And for another thing, I don't like where the incisors are. Can't we move them to where the bicuspids are, and maybe slide this canine tooth more to the front? I'm sorry, Uncle, but this isn't really what I had in mind.'

"That's why you need a strategy."

I love that story. They ought to teach it in Marketing 101.

Then again, I don't know. You'd probably see lots of MBAs walking around with plaid teeth.

Art direction and occasional half-baked philosophy by Stavros Cosmopulos, OFD. His remarks quoted herein are copyrighted, and used with permission.

—CATTLE CALL—

People on the golf course, at cocktail parties, they ask me, "How did you get into this line of work?" Meaning being a broadcast voiceover.

What they usually mean is, How can *I* get into this line of work, where I get to hang out with celebrities and sports legends and have catered lunches at the studios and get things called "residuals.[1]"

I tell people the truth about this.

"I got into it because I could." For the same reason dogs lick various parts of their anatomy. I was often the writer or producer or director of the commercials, so it often fell upon me to do the casting.

My call. My purview. My part.

Not that I can't act. I have a good ear and a whisky baritone, and can read certain styles as well as anyone.

Actually, make that "certain style." Singular. I'm terse, few words, laconic, laid back to just short of comatose. A talk show host once yelled over the phone at me, "Why do you always sound like you're asleep?"

"Maybe it's your programming," I replied with kindness, turning the other cheek to the right-wing pond scum.

Anyway, that style gives me a range from "A" almost all the way to "B." It used to say on my demo reel, "Ray Welch, Man of Many Voice." (Gail calls it "Man of Many Growl.")

[1]Residuals are fresh payments, every 13 weeks, for work you've already recorded. God bless the Screen Actors Guild and the American Federation of Television and Radio Artists.

I tend to write that way, too. For the most part, I hate exclamation points. Hate seeing them, hate hearing them. They're usually artificial loudnesses stuck in there because the writer can't find the right noun or verb, and he's trying to get power out of punctuation marks.

Same with most adjectives and adverbs. They are not our friends, at least when they're in mobs. Is "succulent steer beef simmered to perfection, served with a garden-fresh salad in a zingy-zesty sauce with crumb-crisp croutons!" any better than "steak and salad"? Suppose a friend invites you to dinner and tells you he'll be serving succulent steer beef simmered, etc.... Me, I wouldn't be real hungry.

When he's not writing or directing plays or movies, one of my favorite essayists is David Mamet, author of *Writing in Restaurants*. His sentences have about as many adjectives as his scenes have props. I too write in restaurants. I also read in them. Especially the menus. And laugh, to the point where other patrons start edging away from me. "Soup 'n' Sandwich" is usually a funny chapter. But don't get me started.

The most frequent comment I get from directors, when I'm on the performer side of the glass, is "Can you punch it up a little, Ray, give it more energy?" (In other words, "Can you throw a couple of exclams in there?") To which I want to say, "No, the sentence doesn't call for it." But I'm not proud. So I usually say, "Sure, I'll give it a try."

Orson Welles could get away with that crap, but Senator, you're no Orson Welles.

−CATTLE CALL−

Nor was a guy named Bob Mundy.

Bob was a radio jazz show host, a onetime deejay, a voice-over wannabe. We liked each other. He auditioned with me a lot, and seldom got the part.

Sometimes, when I didn't have a script handy for an actor to read from, I'd use the copy on the back of a Camel pack. It is a stilted piece of writing, but there's still a way to read it so it makes sense.

Dating back to when cigarette brands used to have coupons stuck under the cellophane, good for a penny on your next pack of Raleighs, the copy on the Camel pack said:

Don't look for premiums or coupons, as the cost of the tobaccos blended in CAMEL Cigarettes prohibits the use of them.

A stern warning. (It's still on the back of the pack, by the way, in type half the size of the SURGEON GENERAL'S WARNING.)

So I hand the pack to Mundy and say, "Want to give it a read, for time and level, Bob?"

"Sure," he says, and clears his throat.

"Okay, take one, whenever you're ready."

"Ahem, ahem," he says. And with pipes as loud as a Harley-Davidson's, he booms, "DON'T LOOK FOR PREMIUMS OR COUPONS, AS THE…"

As in, "AT NOON TODAY, THE JAPANESE BOMBED PEARL HARBOR."

We were selling something like ladies' undergarments.

So I said to Bob, "Well, okay, not bad. But how about we back off it a little, make it more conversational. Like you're just giving a friendly tip to a buddy. Even put a few stutters in it. *Ad lib* anything you want. Like, 'Hey, don't even think about looking for coupons or shit, 'cause… 'cause, well, you know what the tobacco in Camels costs, right? 'More like that.' "

"Good direction, Ray."

"All right, here we go on take two, whenever you're ready."

"Ahem, ahem." (Breathe from the diaphragm.) "DON'T LOOK FOR PREMIUMS OR COUPONS, AS THE…"

Now, the pity of it is that Mundy had a voice. One of those Schlitz "Go for the Gusto" voices that makes mine sound like PeeWee Herman's. And he was a smart guy—about jazz, about books, about a lot of things. Things that didn't include making colloquial sense out of formal word units.

A lot of art directors and (especially) graphic designers are that way, too. They have a great eye, just as Mundy had a great voice, but to them words are just graphic elements to be placed on a page where they look good but may not contribute at all to their being understood. Mundy's voice, full of sound and fury, often did the same.

There is no money in reading Camel packs, so I moved on to real scripts, mostly (at least at first) stuff I'd written myself. My debut was a spot for Father Robert Drinan, a Democratic Congressman from Massachusetts whose advertising I'd created for several terms.

Every two years, he squeaked past his Republican opponent, by margins of 49% to 48%, with 3% going to Nevada Bob or someone.

Everyone knew Drinan was competent and honest, but his negatives were many and deep. Voters didn't cotton to priests in Congress. Didn't care much for workaholics. Weren't warm toward Jesuits with a slim sense of humor. Didn't find his dandruff a fashion accent. (Priests in black suit coats are the wrong folks to have dandruff.)

So I wrote this spot that went right after the negatives. Held them up to the light of day and shook them by the shoulders. I liked the concept. Still do.

I forget the exact words but, from the mouth of a blue-collar working stiff, they were something like this:

"I do not like Father Drinan. I don't like priests in Congress. Not where they belong. I don't like the way he gets all preachy about Nixon. I don't like this. I don't like that... But you know what? I'm not voting for the guy because I like him. I'm voting for him because we need him." I had picked an out-of-work screen actor as the voice. One of the reasons he was out of work was a drinking problem. He never showed up at the studio. I recorded the script myself.

Turns out the spot got famous, and I found I'd typecast myself into a blue-collar working stiff. Which didn't hurt with clients like BrandsMart discount stores, Pewter Pot restaurants, and other mass marketers. But I'd never be picked as the spokesman for the Boston Pops.

That's okay. There are more discount stores and coffee shops out there than symphony orchestras.

After I resigned from Welch Currier in 1987, I had some decisions to make. Simple decisions. Like, who the hell am I? What should I put on my resume? Am I a writer, voice talent, political handler, marketing consultant, broadcast director, poker player?

The answer was, "Yes I am."

But that's no good when someone asks you, "Mr. Welch, what exactly do you do?"

So my answer became, "Mr. Smith, what exactly do you need?" It's still my answer.

But my passion at the time was being voice talent. Writing, my first love, is usually hard, sometimes impossible. I think it was Dorothy Parker who said, "Writing is easy; all you have to do is stare at a blank piece of paper until little drops of blood form on your forehead." Amen.

But I get fired up in the studio, on either side of the glass. I like the interplay with the techs, the talent, the copywriters and art directors, and

-CATTLE CALL-

the war stories that most of us have in our bags and share in the studio. But mostly what I like is being the announcer, the storyteller. I'm good at it. I can usually bring enough value-added to the table to get all there is from a script. And sometimes, being a writer as well as a voice, I can make it better than it started out.

So when I left the agency my first steps were to try to make it as an actor, and to hell with writing ads.

I started going to casting calls, something I never had to do when I was the one choosing the talent.

Casting calls are aptly referred to as cattle calls.

You want a herd of actors and announcers to come read for a part? Whether or not they're right for it? Just treat yourself to a cattle call. For $1,000 or $1,500 you can spend all day watching men and women misread lines and suck up to directors. Most of the folks who show are struggling, seldom-employed artists. The ones who don't show usually don't have to. They have agents who have already locked up the part for them. The rest, they're taking a roll of the dice. Forty people on the pass line rolling for two parts. In a spot that's going to net them $330 each, unless the thing goes national or into residuals. So you've got one chance in 20 to land a role.

Make that, I've got one chance in 20.

And the role I'm trying to land at today's cattle call is that of a young would-be homeowner trying to get a mortgage. Well, says the script,

all I need is *The Boston Herald.* If I pick up a copy, or better yet, sub-scribe to the paper, I'll find stuff to help me get a low-cost loan for the house of my dreams.

I'm auditioning for the part of a dude in his mid-twenties, to whom a dozen extra dollars a month in his mortgage payment is the difference between the American Dream and living on the street in a box.

Now, it would seem to me that if the target demographic is someone in his twenties, maybe a guy around 50 isn't quite right for the part. And did I mention this is an on-camera gig? I don't say a word, just per-form the video.

Which is this:

1. Talent yanks front doorknob to house of dreams.
2. Door won't open. Talent jiggles knob.
3. Talent kicks door.
4. Talent places foot against door and pulls hard.
5. Talent places both feet against door and pulls hard.
6. Talent smiles at camera.

We have some problems here.

The first one is a marketing conundrum. If the target is kids in their twenties, why are they casting a man on maybe the 16th hole of his life as the icon? To me, this makes very small sense.

—CATTLE CALL—

And do they really expect me to hang from the doorknob, with both feet up against the door at chest level, and "pull hard"? Do they have an Emergency Medical Team standing by with stretchers and electrical paddles?

And while I'm turning blue, gasping for air, what do they want me to do? They want me to *smile*. At the camera. With my carotid arteries about to burst.

This is going to sell more *Heralds*? Witnessing me explode on camera?

If I thought it might, I may have tried. As it was, all I could do was laugh. Which amused the Casting Director. (Laughter being contagious.)

"Why are you laughing, Mr. Welch?"

I said, "That's the way I promised myself I'd die."

I wobbled down the three flights back to my car and drove to the next session, a call for a made-for-television movie. Okay, I thought. This is where I belong. Drama. People like me.

Not exactly.

The people calling the shots were three ruddy-faced fat men, the show's director, producer, and someone who brought them doughnuts. All of them wore Ascots and affected English accents. Even Doughnut Boy.

"How are you, old lad?" the director said to me.

"Did you say 'How old are you, lad?' "

"No, I said, 'How are you, old sod.' "

"Swell."

"Jolly good. Did you get that from Bogart?"

"Get what from Bogart?"

"Swell."

"What's swell? You mean swollen? My cheek's always like this."

My memory peters out at this point, but the scene drifts back from time to time, as sort of a dream sequence, when I'm dozing off or running a temperature.

"Never mind, chap. We'll just trot along with the audition, if it's all gamey, eh?"

"What's all gamey? The food?"

"Clever boy," he said. By now neither of us knew what the hell the other was trying to say.

He said something like, "Mildred, how's by pulling the coddle on Mr. Welch and furping his thumble, shall we?"

–CATTLE CALL–

Mildred strode over to a table stacked with manila file folders, probably the thumbles, and furped through them. Each file contained a list of
names, people like me, summoned by these crypto-Englishmen to try
out for their made-for-TV movie about which none of us actors knows
a damn thing.

The files had big black felt-tip marker labels on their covers.

One said LEADING MAN.

Another said OLDER BROTHER.

Maybe we were getting somewhere. I could see myself in such a role.
Either of them. Or in something labeled SENSITIVE VICTIMIZED MAN.
"You got a file with that label, old whacker?"

But no. The role they wanted me to read for came from a folder labeled
SLEAZE.

They were casting for two different characters: a pimp and a john.
Right off quick they pegged me for the john.

The john drives up to this hooker and says, "Hey, baby, you want some
action?" That's my line: "Hey, baby, you want some action?" Try and
milk it.

As I studied the script, trying to memorize it, the director said, "Any
queries, old chum?"

"What's my motivation?" Trying to be sarcastic.

He answered me solemnly. "You are horny."

"Good direction," I said.

"So, shall we forthwigger?"

"Is that like 'boogie'?"

"One supposes."

"Then, let's forthwigger."

"Take one," he said, and nodded to the cameraman, a kid in his teens. "Three, two, and... ACTION!"

Now, there is no need to go through that "Three, two, and... ACTION!" bullshit unless you're shooting film, with a clapper, to synch-sound the scenes. But we're shooting tape here, with a home video camera that probably costs less than yours, and this Angloid has everything but a megaphone to cue the massed churls about to launch their arrows from the parapets, and I think I notice he has a hard-on.

Trooper that I am, I rip into my line:

"Hey, baby, looking for some... action?"

—CATTLE CALL—

"CUT," he yells. There was little need to yell CUT, as that one line was the entirety of my scene. At least he didn't have the megaphone. "You blew the line, old scrote. It's supposed to be "Hey, baby, you *want* some action?""

"I know. I was improvising. Seemed more in character."

"It is not more in character. I spent months developing that persona, and I assure you he would never, not in a million years, say 'looking for' some action. Now, shall we breach it one more time?"

"Why not."

"All right, then, there's a good lad… Three, two, and… ACTION!"

"Hi, my name is Ray," I growled. "You come here often?"

Damn Brits have no sense of humor. Even crypto-Brits.

When the dream sequence fades to black, I think maybe I'll just go back to commercials. Ones I write myself. Ones I do the casting for. I'd have me a chance then, I would.

On the drive home, I ponder this acting life. Hobnobbing with English-type folks, up close and personal with nitwits who want me to hang like a bat from a doorknob and smile at the camera. And as I pull into the

driveway, I rehearse my entering line, the one I shall use on Gail (assuming I can get the damn door open) as I swagger into the living room:

"Hey, baby," I breathe from the diaphragm, "you want some action?"

Art Direction / Jim Amadeo

Cattle Call Redux

Back when I was shuffling and dealing out chapters of *Copywriter* to my favorite art directors, I sent "Cattle Call" to both Jim Amadeo and Pete Favat on a "what do you think?" mission. Neither of them thought enough about it to respond by deadline time, so I e–mailed them gentle reminders that began with "DEAR PROCRASTINATING BASTARDS." Finally, Amadeo sent me the version you just read, and I kind of blew off Favat. Until he sent me his take on the story, along with a note saying, "What do you think?" What I thought was, "What the hell kind of book would have two chapters, with the same copy, that look nothing at all alike?" Apparently, this kind of book.

—Ray Welch

cocktail
l you get
g being a

low can I
e I get to
ports leg-
t the stu-
uals."
nis.
" For the
parts of
writer or
nercials,
casting.

short of
e yelled
do you
"

ing," I
e other
n.
a range
"B". It
, "Ray
il calls

For the
points.
them.
nesses

Interesting cocktail,

CATTLE CALL

OUCH
golf cou
cocktail
ties, the
me, "Ho
you get
this lin
work
Mean
being a b
cast voice
What
usually
is, How
get into
line of
where I g
hang out
celebrities
sports leg
and

240

CATTLE CALL

By Ray Welch

PEOPLE on the golf course, at cocktail parties, they ask me, "How did you get into this line of work?" Meaning being a broadcast voiceover.

What they usually mean is, How can I get into this line of work, where I get to hang out with celebrities and sports legends and have catered lunches at the studios and get things called "residuals."

I tell people the truth about this.

"I got into it because I could." For the same reason dogs lick various parts of their anatomy. I was often the writer or producer or director of the commercials, so it often fell upon me to do the casting.

My call. My purview. My part.

Not that I can't act. I have a good ear and a whisky baritone, and can read certain styles as well as anyone.

Actually, make that "certain style." Singular. I'm terse, few words, laconic, laid back to just short of comatose. A talk show host once yelled over the phone at me, "Why do you always sound like you're asleep?"

"Maybe it's your programming," I replied with kindness, turning the other cheek to the right-wing pond scum.

that style gives me a range

WASSUP on
parties, they a
into this line c
broadcast voi

What they
get into this l
hang out wit
ends and have
dios and get t
I tell peop

Ray Welc
My call.
Not that I
and a whisk
tain styles a
Actually,
Singular.
short of con
yelled over
you always

from "A" almost all the way to "B". It used to say on my demo reel, "Ray Welch, Man of Many Voice." (Gail calls it "Man of Many Growl.")

I tend to write that way, too. For the most part, I hate exclamation points. Hate seeing them, hate hearing them. They're usually artificial loudnesses stuck in there because

the writer can't find the right noun or verb, and he's trying to get power out of punctuation marks.

Same with most adjectives and adverbs. They are not our friends, at least when they're in mobs. Is "succulent steer beef simmered to perfection, served with a garden-fresh salad in a zingy-zesty sauce with crumb-crisp croutons!" any better than "steak and salad"? Suppose a friend invites you to dinner and tells you he'll be serving succulent steer beef simmered, etc… Me, I wouldn't be real hungry.

When he's not writing or directing plays or movies, one of my favorite essayists is David Mamet, author of Writing in Restaurants. His sentences have about as many adjectives as his scenes have props. I too write in restaurants. I also read in them. Especially the menus. And laugh, to the point where other patrons start edging away from me. "Soup 'n' Sandwich" is usually a funny chapter. But don't get me started.

• • •

THE MOST FREQUENT comment I get from directors, when I'm on the performer side of the glass, is "Can you punch it up a little, Ray, give it more energy?" (In other words, "Can you

CLOCK

FUSE

You ca
situati
Plugm

energy?" (In other words, "Can you throw a couple of exclams in there?") To which I want to say, "No, the sentence doesn't call for it." But I'm not proud. So I usually say, "Sure, I'll give it a try."

Orson Welles could get away with that crap, but Senator, you're no Orson Welles.

Nor was a guy named Bob Mundy.

Bob was a radio jazz show host, a onetime deejay, a voiceover wannabe. We liked each other. He auditioned with me a lot, and seldom got the part.

Sometimes, when I didn't have a script handy for an actor to read from, I'd use the copy on the back of a Camel pack. It is a stilted piece of writing, but there's still a way to read it so it makes sense.

Dating back to when cigarette brands used to have coupons stuck under the cellophane, good for a penny on your next pack of Raleighs, the copy on the Camel pack said:

Don't look for premiums or coupons, as the cost of the tobaccos blended in CAMEL Cigarettes prohibits the use of them.

A stern warning. (It's still on the back of the pack, by the way, in type half the size of the SURGEON GENERAL'S WARNING.)

243

SCRAPE, NO S

O WEAR AND

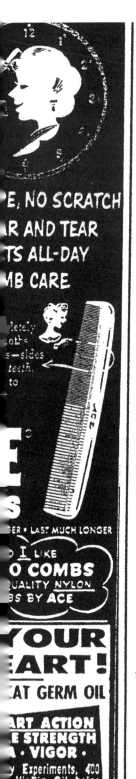
So I hand the pack to Mundy and say, "Want to give it a read, for time and level, Bob?"

"Sure," he says, and clears his throat.

"Okay, take one, whenever you're ready."

"Ahem, ahem," he says. And with pipes as loud as a Harley-Davidson's, he booms, "DON'T LOOK FOR PREMIUMS OR COUPONS, AS THE..."

As in, "AT NOON TODAY, THE JAPANESE BOMBED PEARL HARBOR."

We were selling something like ladies' undergarments.

So I said to Bob, "Well, okay, not bad. But how about we back off it a little, make it more conversational. Like you're just giving a friendly tip to a buddy. Even put a few stutters in it. Ad lib anything you want. Like, 'Hey, don't even think about looking for coupons or shit, 'cause...cause, well, you know what the tobacco in Camels costs, right?.' More like that."

"Good direction, Ray."

"All right, here we go on take two, whenever you're ready."

"Ahem, ahem." (Breathe from the diaphragm.) "DON'T LOOK FOR PREMIUMS OR COUPONS, AS THE..."

Now, the pity of it is that Mundy had a voice. One of those Schlitz "Go for the Gusto" voices that makes mine sound like PeeWee Herman's. And he was a smart guy—about jazz, about books, about a lot of things. Things that didn't include making colloquial sense out of formal word units.

A lot of art directors and (especially) graphic designers are that way, too. They have a great eye, just as Mundy had a great voice, but to them words are just graphic elements to be placed on a page

245

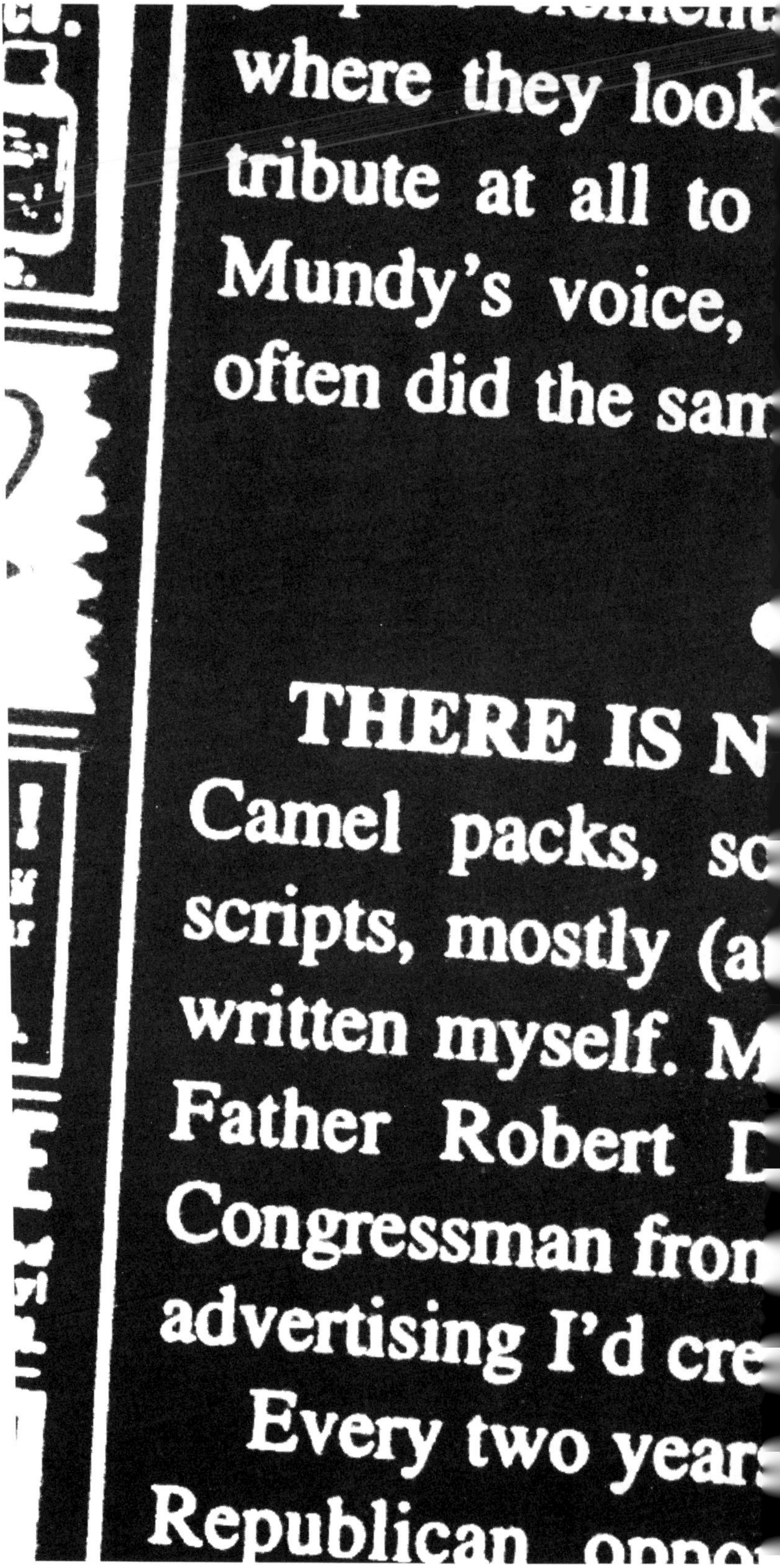

where they look
tribute at all to
Mundy's voice,
often did the sam

THERE IS N

Camel packs, sc
scripts, mostly (a
written myself. M
Father Robert D
Congressman fron
advertising I'd cre
Every two year:
Republican oppo

graphic elements to be placed on a page where they look good but may not contribute at all to their being understood. Mundy's voice, full of sound and fury, often did the same.

• • •

THERE IS NO MONEY in reading Camel packs, so I moved on to real scripts, mostly (at least at first) stuff I'd written myself. My debut was a spot for Father Robert Drinan, a Democratic Congressman from Massachusetts whose advertising I'd created for several terms.

Every two years, he squeaked past his Republican opponent, by margins of 49% to 48%, with 3% going to Nevada Bob or someone.

So I hand the p
"Want to give it
level, Bob?"
"Sure," he says.

Bob, "Well, okay
about we back off
conversational. Lil
friendly tip to a b
stutters in it. Ad l
Like, 'Hey, don't (
ing for coupons o
well, you know
Camels costs, righ
"Good direction
"All right, here
whenever you're r
"Ahem, ahem.'

Beverly

Herman's. And h
about jazz, about
things. Things that
colloquial sense
units.

A lot of art dire
graphic designers

247

Everyone knew Drinan was competent and honest, but his negatives were many and deep. Voters didn't cotton to priests in Congress. Didn't care much for workaholics. Weren't warm toward Jesuits with a slim sense of humor. Didn't find his dandruff a fashion accent. (Priests in black suit coats are the wrong folks to have dandruff.)

So I wrote this spot that went right after the negatives. Held them up to the light of day and shook them by the shoulders. I liked the concept. Still do.

I forget the exact words but, from the mouth of a blue-collar working stiff, they were something like this:

"I do not like Father Drinan. I don't like priests in Congress. Not where they belong. I don't like the way he gets all preachy about Nixon. I don't like this. I don't like that... But you know what? I'm not voting for the guy because I like him. I'm voting for him because we need him."

I had picked an out-of-work screen actor as the voice. One of the reasons he was out of work was a drinking problem. He never showed up the studio. I recorded the script myself.

Turns out the spot got famous, and I found I'd typecast myself into a blue-collar working stiff. Which didn't hurt with clients like BrandsMart discount stores, Pewter Pot restaurants, and other mass marketers. But I'd never be picked as the spokesman for the Boston Pops.

That's okay. There are more discount stores and coffee shops out there than symphony orchestras.

• • •

248

AFTER I RESIGNED from Welch Currier in 1987, I had some decisions to make. Simple decisions. Like, who the hell am I? What should I put on my resume? Am I a writer, voice talent, political handler, marketing consultant, broadcast director, poker player?

The answer was, Yes I am.

But that's no good when someone asks you, "Mr. Welch, what exactly do you do?"

So my answer became, "Mr. Smith, what exactly do you need?" It's still my answer.

But my passion at the time was being voice talent. Writing, my first love, is usually hard, sometimes impossible. I think it was Dorothy Parker who said, "Writing is easy; all you have to do is stare at a blank piece of paper until little drops of blood form on your forehead." Amen.

But I get fired up in the studio, on either side of the glass. I like the interplay with the techs, the talent, the copywriters and art directors, and the war stories that most of us have in our bags and share in the studio. But mostly what I like is being the announcer, the storyteller. I'm good at it. I can usually bring enough value-added to the table to get all there is from a script. And sometimes, being a writer as well as a voice, I can make it better than it started out.

So when I left the agency my first steps were to try to make it as an actor, and to hell with writing ads.

I started going to casting calls, some-thing I never had to do when I was the one choosing the talent.

Casting calls are aptly referred to as cattle calls.

You want a herd of actors and announcers to come read for a part? Whether or not they're right for it? Just treat yourself to a cattle call. For $1,000 or $1,500 you can spend all day watching men and women misread lines and suck up to directors. Most of the folks who show are struggling, seldom-employed artists. The ones who don't show usually don't have to. They have agents who have already locked up the part for them. The rest, they're taking a roll of the dice. Forty people on the pass line rolling for two parts. In a spot that's going to net them $330 each, unless the thing goes national or into residuals. So you've got one chance in 20 to land a role.

Make that, I've got one chance in 20.

And the role I'm trying to land at today's cattle call is that of a young would-be homeowner trying to get a mortgage. Well, says the script, all I need is the *Boston*

Herald. If I pick up a copy, or better yet, subscribe to the paper, I'll find stuff to help me get a low-cost loan for the house of my dreams.

I'm auditioning for the part of a dude in his mid-twenties, to whom a dozen dollars a month in his mortgage payment is the difference between the American Dream and living in the street in a box.

Now, it would seem to me that if the target demographic is someone in his twenties, maybe a guy around 50 isn't quite right for the part. And did I mention this is an on-camera gig? I don't say a word, just perform the video.

Which is this:

1. Talent yanks front doorknob to house of dreams.
2. Door won't open. Talent jiggles knob.
3. Talent kicks door.
4. Talent places foot against door and pulls hard.
5. Talent places both feet against door and pulls hard.
6. Talent smiles at camera.

We have some problems here. The first one is a marketing conundrum. If the target is kids in their twenties, why are they casting a man on maybe the 1(

250

hole of his life as the icon? To me, this makes very small sense.

And do they really expect me to hang from the doorknob, with both feet up against the door at chest level, and "pull hard"? Do they have an Emergency Medical Team standing by with stretchers and electrical paddles?

And while I'm turning blue, gasping for air, what do they want me to do? They want me to smile. At the camera. With my carotid arteries about to burst.

This is going to sell more Heralds? Witnessing me explode on camera?

If I thought it might, I may have tried. As it was, all I could do was laugh. Which amused the Casting Director. (Laughter being contagious.)

"Why are you laughing, Mr. Welch?"

I said, "That's the way I promised myself I'd die."

I wobbled down the three flights back to my car and drove to the next session, a call for a made-for-television movie. Okay, I thought. This is where I belong. Drama. People like me.

Not exactly.

The people calling the shots were three ruddy-faced fat men, the show's director, producer, and

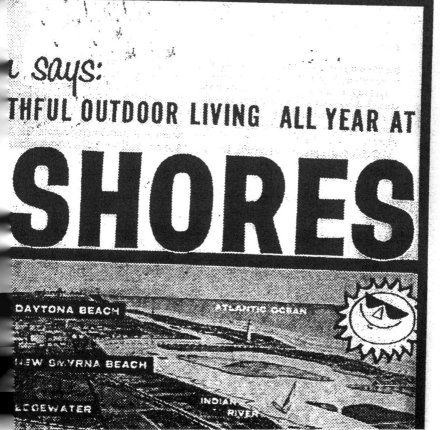

u says:

THFUL OUTDOOR LIVING ALL YEAR AT

SHORES

DAYTONA BEACH   ATLANTIC OCEAN

NEW SMYRNA BEACH

EDGEWATER   INDIAN RIVER

251

someone who brought them doughnuts. All of them wore Ascots and affected English accents. Even Doughnut Boy.

"How are you, old lad?" the director said to me.

"Did you say How old are you, lad?"

"No, I said how are you, old sod."

"Swell."

"Jolly good. Did you get that from Bogart?"

"Get what from Bogart?"

"Swell."

"What's swell? You mean swollen? My cheek's always like this."

My memory peters out at this point, but the scene drifts back from time to time, as sort of a dream sequence, when I'm dozing off or running a tempera- ture.

"Never mind, chap. We'll just trot along with the audition, if it's all gamey, eh?"

"If what's all gamey? The food?"

"Clever boy," he said. By now neither of knew what the hell the other was trying to say. He said something like,

"Mildred, how's by pulling the coddle on Mr. Welch and furp- ing his thumble, shall we?"

Mildred strode over to a table stacked with manila file folders, probably the thumbles, and furped through them. Each file contained a list of names, people like me, summoned by these crypto-Englishmen to try out of for their made-for-TV movie about which none of us actors knows a damn thing.

The files had big black felt- tip marker labels on their cov- ers.

One said LEADING MAN.

Another said OLDER BROTHER.

Maybe we were getting somewhere. I could see myself in such a role. Either of them Or in something labeled SEN- SITIVE VICTIMIZED MAN. "You got a file with that label, old whacker?"

But no. The role they want- ed me to read for came from a folder labeled SLEAZE.

They were casting for two different characters: a pimp and a john. Right off quick they pegged me for the john.

The john goes up to this hooker and says, "Hey, baby, you want some action?" That's my line: "Hey, baby, you want some action?" Try and milk it.

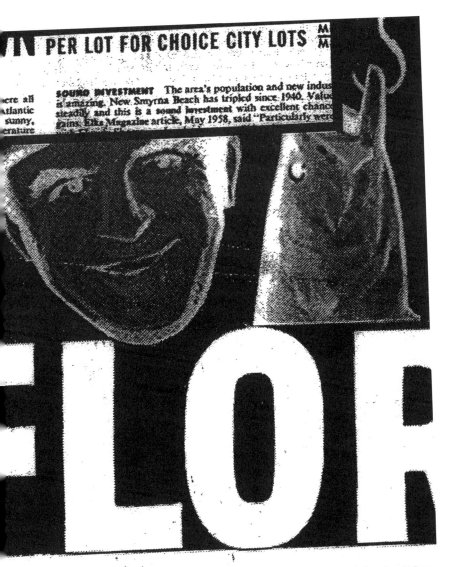

PER LOT FOR CHOICE CITY LOTS

SOUND INVESTMENT The area's population and new indus is amazing. New Smyrna Beach has tripled since 1940. Value steadily and this is a sound investment with excellent chance gains. Elks Magazine article, May 1958, said "Particularly were

ere all
Atlantic
sunny,
erature

FLOR

JACKSONVILLE

LOCATI

IS EVERYT

BEACH
A BEACH
DGEWATER

FLORIDA
SHORES

As I studied the script, trying to memorize it, the director said, "Any queries, old chum?"

"What's my motivation?" Trying to be sarcastic.

He answered me solemnly. "You are horny."

"Good direction," I said.

"So, shall we forthwigger?"

"Is that like 'boogie'?"

"One supposes."

"Then, let's forthwigger."

"Take one," he said, and nodded to the cameraman, a kid in his teens. "Three, two, and...ACTION!"

Now, there is no need to go through that "Three, two, and...ACTION!" bullshit unless you're shooting film, with a clapper, to synch-sound the scenes. But we're shooting tape here, with a home video camera that probably costs less than yours, and this Angloid has everything but a megaphone to cue the massed churls about to launch their arrows from the parapets, and I think I notice he has a hard-on.

Trooper that I am, I rip into my line:

"Hey, baby, looking for some...action?"

"CUT," he yells. There was little need to yell CUT, as that one line was the entirety of my scene. At least he didn't have the megaphone. "You blew the line, old scrote. It's supposed to be 'Hey, baby, you want some action?'"

"I know. I was improvising. Seemed more in character."

"It is not more in character. I spent months developing that persona, and I assure you, he would never, not in a million years, say 'looking for' some action. Now, shall we breach it one more time?"

"Why not."

"All right, then, there's a good lad... Three, two, and...ACTION!"

"Hi, my name is Ray," I growled. "You come here often?"

Damn Brits have no sense of humor. Even crypto-Brits.

When the dream sequence fades to black, I think maybe I'll just go back to commercials. Ones I write myself. Ones I do the casting for. I'd have me a chance then, I would.

• • •

ON THE DRIVE HOME, I ponder this acting life. Hobnobbing with English-type folks, up close and personal with nitwits who want me to hang like a bat from a doorknob and smile at the camera. And as I pull into the driveway, I rehearse my entering line, the one I shall use on Gail (assuming I can get the damn door open) as I swagger into the living room:

"Hey, baby," I breathe from the diaphragm, "you want some action?"

END

Favat, Grady Arrested

BOSTON Pete Favat and Kevin Grady were arrested early Sunday morning after

Cronies

Photos by Susan Rankin, Design by John Housley

Yes, it's actually
owned by a guy
named Aidan.
With brogue and all.
He has no plans to
turn it into a chain.

After three years in our new town, I have made cronies.

The last cronies I had were 10 or 20 years ago, when my business partner and I and a few other ad people used to hang out at some bar on Boylston Street and either bitch about the industry or conspire to dominate it.

Cronies are different from friends. You get to be a friend only after years, usually after shared pain or adventures and proof of purchase.

You get to be a crony faster, by buying a drink. Or having a shared interest. It can be golf or local politics or movies or the hotel on Hope Street that some folks are trying to get the Town to let them renovate.

It's not that simple, but you get the idea.

Cronies are cheap substitutes for friends. You don't have to invest a whole lot. But in a pinch, or given that all your real friends still live back in Boston or in California or some other damn place, cronies are pure gold—at a discount price.

Around here, the place we buy each other drinks is Aidan's, an Irish pub in Bristol, on the Rhode Island coast halfway between Providence and Newport.

The hotel my cronies want to buy and re-hab is the Beaumont, an antique eyesore on Hope

Street. Potential for 55 rooms, restaurant, a couple of bars, and a rooftop lounge with a drop-dead view of Bristol Harbor. Plus ample parking, simply by blowing up three or four neighboring structures. It's potentially a first-rate joint, if you gut it and pour more money into it than you will ever make back in a million years.

But the boys didn't get into this solely for profit. Partly they cared a whole lot about Bristol. Partly they were crazy. My new cronies.

Let me introduce them:[1]

Tom Whiteside. Rhode Island boy, Brown University class of '56 or so, business background. Front man for the Beaumont group, snappy dresser if you like tweeds. A little slick but totally charming. Whiteside drinks Manhattans.

John Piper. Former bank exec, Treasurer of the group. John and I went to Dartmouth together — in different decades, but giving us a jumpstart on cronyism. Old Thumper Ale.

Manuel Montiero. Or if you look fast, a Portuguese Robert DeNiro with a short beard. Tough little bastard. Born in Bristol, moved away, made a fortune, returned at age 55 to spread some good and a fair amount of influence. Montiero's big word is "respect," and you don't want to go there with him unless you understand that the term "a fucking gentleman" is a sincere and high compliment.

[1] I've changed the names here. Because in Rhode Island, from time to time, a body has been known to wash up on the beach. "Poor man, he was just out for a walk when he got caught in the current."

There are others that I got to know. Maintenance men, painters, a man with a shovel and no teeth except one, and a chemist who invents stuff that keeps down the stench of landfills made of decaying quahog shells.

Montiero is the brains of the bunch. Not by dint of college, but by way of street smarts. The book on Manny is that he gains access by side doors, plays all his cards face up, and keeps his word. You do not want Montiero as an enemy. At least I don't.

You'd think that after three years this group of seasoned businessmen could get permission from the Town to buy and renovate an old firetrap hotel. What could go wrong?

I will tell you what could go wrong.

Bristol is one of the most gracious towns on the Rhode Island coast. Its streets are clean. Its beaches are maintained. There's plenty of public land, like Colt State Park, with walking trails and bike paths, and hundreds of acres along the seaside. There's a downtown historic district. People mow their lawns and paint their houses. There are signs that say, "Private Property, Public Welcome." (That's the one that made Gail and me want to come live here.)

If every town had this kind of attitude, you'd never see a beer bottle on the side of the road.

This is the
hotel the
Town so
assiduously
seeks to
protect in
its pristine
originality.

KEEP OUT

Like it or not, maintaining the character of the town requires some bureaucracy. A Planning Board, an Historical Society, a Town Council, a Zoning Commission, old busybodies at the barbershop, and decades of grudges to honor. In a small town, it's the price you pay for preservation.

To get building permits and approvals you have to deal with all of the above. For years, some or all of them have hobbled the Hotel Beaumont development.

So what are my cronies doing about it?

Piper makes business plans to prove the project is viable. Whiteside badgers someone new every day at Town Hall. Montiero lines up his ducks by side door or telephone, *sotto voce*. And the result is stalemate.

Montiero's friends mistrust Whiteside, the consummate Republican WASP. Whiteside's friends don't know how to deal with Montiero, the only one in the bunch who knows how to pronounce a Portuguese surname (in a town that's 60% Portuguese). Piper isn't even a Bristolian—he's from high-rent Barrington up the road —so you can imagine how much clout he's got in our Town government. Same result: deadlock.

So, as I see my duty, there is only one thing to do. I must save the project.

That's what a citizen does for his town. That's what a man does for his cronies.

As a copywriter with 23 political campaigns under my belt and acumen they still talk about at the Parker House Bar in Boston, I figured I'd write a letter to the editor of the local weekly, the *Bristol Phoenix*. This was two weeks before the Town elections.

Before I sent the letter I went to Aidan's and, as a courtesy, ran it past Whiteside and Piper. "Swell," they said. Montiero wasn't there, so I called him. No answer, no voicemail, but what the hell. What could he object to.

Here is the letter. It ran Thursday. (Today is Saturday.)

To the Editor:

Me, I'm a carpetbagger. Born in Boston, lived there 50 years, discovered Bristol by accident three years ago, fell in love with it, bought a house, and plan to die here.

Bristol's my home. I mean to treat it as such.

So as a citizen, when I see something stupid going on in my town, I feel obliged to speak up about it. And what I see with the Hotel Beaumont is about as stupid as it gets.

Here you have a fleabag hotel, a blight on Hope Street, and Tom Whiteside and some other businesspeople want to fix it up, return it to its original splendor, okay? They draw up plans that make sense to the bankers, the Historical Society, the neighbors, to everyone else in Bristol...

Everyone except the Town Council. Ever since I've lived here they've done nothing but lay land mines to delay or prevent the restoration of the Beaumont. And I used to think the Boston City Council was inept.

Come on, guys. Approve the damn plans. Or do we always want an abandoned flophouse in the center of town?

Other than as a citizen, who might want to invest effort or money here, I have no vested interest in the project. I met Whiteside a year ago at Aidan's and bought him a drink (which is what Democrats always seem to do for Republicans). But this isn't about Whiteside, or even about politics. It's about Bristol. It's about my town. And by the way, elections are coming up.

Ray Welch

There, the good citizen thought to himself. Not a bad letter. I even got a little political humor into it. Folks will smile and I will be popular.

Peter Valachi had no smile in his voice when he called me about seven minutes after the *Phoenix* hit the newsstands on Thursday.

The only Valachi I'd ever heard of was a Mafia hit man in the 1960s who ratted out some crime family in a RICO plea bargain.

This particular Valachi was a member of the Bristol Town Council who said to my voicemail that he'd appreciate my calling him to discuss some of the points raised by my letter. He left his pager number.

I got the message after a midday golf game and called him.

We had a short, civil conversation. In which the words "slimy" and "lying little turd" were used only sparingly. It appeared that Valachi and Whiteside were not close buddies. They were certainly not cronies.

The Council, it seemed, was not amused by my allegations of foot-dragging. Nor was it fond of "land mines." To the contrary, Valachi said, the Council I had maligned had done everything humanly possible to speed along the project. To grease it. In fact there was going to be a vote, probably next week, probably to approve it.

That is, until my letter appeared. And shit started flying. "You have created a hornets nest at the Town Hall" is how Valachi described it. And a vote that had appeared to be a lock was now up for grabs. I think "dead meat" were his words. There was now not a single member of the Council who could vote "yea" on the Beaumont without looking as if he'd caved under the pressure of the press. Shamed into it. By a rabble-rousing carpetbagger.

As I contemplated these things and my newfound popularity, Gail said, "I'm going for a walk. Don't drink too much."

Minutes later a large Mercedes pulled into the driveway. The doorbell rang. Two gentlemen in suits. One of them was Manuel Montiero.

"We were in the neighborhood," he said. "Do you have a minute? Or is this a bad time."

Well, I had just gotten off the course, dressed in shorts and a sweat-soaked polo shirt, shoeless, four days of stubble on my face. My back was killing me, I was running a fever, and my new blood pressure medications had me feeling faint.

"Not at all," I said. "Please come in. I'm honored, Manuel."

And I really was.

Manny introduced me to his friend, a distinguished-looking man in his sixties who was doing some sort of deal with Montiero, unrelated to the Beaumont. Just driving around the neighborhood talking business, I guess, when they happened to be passing my house, which is on a cul de sac leading nowhere.

"You have a very nice home," Manny said. "It speaks well of you."

"Thank you," I said. "Can I get you guys a drink?"

Manny said maybe a little vodka, any brand, and some ice. His friend wouldn't mind a cup of coffee. I was already working on a scotch and soda to wash down a giant painkiller pill for my back spasms.

We took our drinks out to the back deck. It is pretty much out of sight from the neighbors, and far enough away so you can use vile language without being overheard. Manny and I lighted cigarettes.

"May I speak frankly?" he said.

"Yes."

"Okay, for one thing, this meeting never happened."

"What meeting?" I said.

"This meeting," said the friend.

"As I just said, what meeting." Proving I knew how to play the game. (I later heard Manny tell a confederate, "John, John, don't worry; Raymond is no rookie.")

"Then I'll get to the point," said Manny.

"You have fucked things up beyond belief." He stood at the railing, admiring the roses, as my popularity soared to new heights. "But don't take that harshly. There may be ways to un-fuck them."

"Does this have anything to do with a Mr. Valachi?"

"Oh my God, he's already talked to you?"

"Ten minutes ago. I get the feeling he's been elected by the Council to express its opinion in this matter."

"Yeah, you could say he's head honcho of the hornets nest."

But how did Manny already know about this? Why didn't he call before he "stopped by"? How did he even know I'd be home? Could he have talked with Valachi by car phone a few minutes ago?

All irrelevant. Montiero gets things done.

What's relevant is that for weeks it's been Montiero alone, using his side doors and *sotto voce,* who's been lining up his ducks, orchestrating all the machinations leading to a "yea" vote. Quietly court-ing each Councilman, cashing in chips, finding ways for everyone to save face, be a hero. A Bristolian camel broker sitting under a blanket.

I said to him, "Manny, you should have been born an Arab, not a Portugee. Please take that as a compliment."

"I take it as such, thank you. Now here's how you can help un-fuck things."

It was getting chilly out on the deck, so we went to my first-floor den, a room where you could close off two glass-paneled doors and smoke cigarettes without stinking up the house. From where Manny's friend sat, he could see through one of the doors out to the driveway and the front walk.

"Hold it," he stage-whispered. "Someone's coming!"

Sweet Jesus, I said to myself, it must be Valachi, come to gun me down! I damn near dropped to the floor.

It was Gail at the door, back from her walk. "Anyone like more coffee?" she asked.

But back to Manny's plan. He suggested, strongly, that I call Valachi back and tell him that I've had an epiphany, that I now see how hard and effectively the Council has worked to move this project forward. Against all odds. And I should write a letter of apology and have it hand-delivered tomorrow morning to all five members of the Council. And I should write a new Letter to the Editor for next week's *Phoenix,* totally reversing my field. And...

"Respectfully, Manuel, I have an alternative idea. Sure, I'll write another letter saying that

I went off a little half-cocked, that sort of thing. But right now, with your permission.... Do you know Mr. Valachi's direct line, off the top of your head?"

He did.

I dialed Valachi on the speakerphone, told him Manny and his friend were with me, and said, "Hey, maybe I came on too strong. Sorry if I offended you guys."

"Thank you, Mr. Welch. I'll pass that along to the other members." (So much for the five hand-delivered letters of apology.)

"Good. And could you do me a favor?"

"If it's within my legal power."

"Please tell Mr. Montiero to put the pistol back in his pocket."

Three hours after his asking "do you have a minute?" Manny and his friend said goodbye. Montiero looked me in the eyes, took my shoulders, and said, "Thank you, Ray. You are a fucking gentleman."

Yesterday afternoon, Friday, right before the hotel proposal passed, Manny hand-delivered my second letter to the *Phoenix,* then summoned Whiteside and Piper to a meeting. Apparently it was a Come-to-Jesus meeting.

Montiero lit into them, saying that because they knew (and I didn't) that the deal had
been brokered days ago, then my letter could only
come back to bite them—and me. It could do no
possible good—the timing was terrible—but it had
the potential to queer the whole deal. Worse, said
Montiero, it would make Ray Welch look like a fool
or a pawn. In short, Ray would be taking the fall for
them.

"This is not the respect you show a new
friend," he said.

Last night I got calls from both Whiteside and Piper.

They were emotional calls. Genuine.
Whiteside said he was physically ill when he
realized how his blithe okay of the letter could lead
to trouble for me. They never meant me harm—me
"of all people."

I told them, hey, I'm a big boy, I can take
my lumps. Besides, I volunteered for this mission;
you guys never asked me to write the damn letter.

Makes no difference, they said. We let you
down. You don't do that to friends.

I haven't been to Aidan's today. But it's almost
noon, so maybe I'll take a drive down, try and hook up with
a couple of cronies.

Manny Montiero,
traveling incognito.
This picture actually
makes him look taller
than he is.

"The Boys at Aidan's Bar"

by Ken Maryanski.

Kenny met some

of my cronies.

I have no comment.

None whatsoever.

"There are more felons per square foot here than anyplace else in Bristol," Manny Montiero said to me, looking around the bar. "But they're my felons."

Over the mirror were booze bottles I'd never seen before. I recognized Seagram's 7 on the top shelf, along with a loudspeaker and a crucifix.

"I'll have a dry Beefeater martini with a twist," I said.

The bartender looked at Manny in Portuguese. He said something filled with "zsj" sounds, pointed at me, pointed at the bar, and flung his arms out. Manny patted him on the arm and said, "Gin."

The bartender rummaged through bottles and pulled out an Old Mister Boston brand, poured four ounces into a pilsner glass, added three ice cubes, and set it down in front of me, pleased with his handiwork. "That's as close as you're going to come at the Portugee Club," Manny said.

"Grazie," I said to the bartender.

He looked at me funny.

"Obrigado," Manny said. "Grazie is Italian. In Portugee it's obrigado."

"Obligato," I tried.

"That's Japanese. You don't need the 'o' on the end."

"Arrigato is Japanese. I mean what the hell, I'm trying to say thank you. Anything close ought to do."

Two black-bearded men stared at me from across the room. Everyone in the room, about 15 men, had a black beard, or heavy black whiskers, at least. And except for Tony, the other bartender, and Louie, the old man with the gold chronograph, they all stayed strictly to Portuguese, lest the strange Anglo should hear something incriminating.

The language sounds something like Italian with random "zsj" sounds thrown in, plus the occasional English word for clarification.

"Como zsj fucking dice al dorzsj?"

"Si, el contradillo zsj no bono. No fucking bono, cocksucker. Zsj."

Manny told me there's a high place in the Pyrenees where the Portuguese and Spanish both speak the same ancient Romance language--neither Portuguese, nor Spanish, but some fusion of both. Maybe it's what they spoke before splitting off into different countries. Like Italy.

As long as I'm teaching you Portuguese, let me tell you about "cocksucker." It is used as punctuation, an aside, a social comment. You can sort of sprinkle it into sentences anywhere you wish, and it modifies whatever you want it to. For example, "I watch Santo cross the street, cocksucker, anna Chevy come screamin rounda conna wit tree kids in it, coxucker." This is acceptable Queen's usage.

Manny tells me the diphthong "th" sound doesn't exist in Portuguese. (Just as the "r" sound doesn't exist, except where it shouldn't, in Bostonese.) Which accounts for "wit tree kids." But accounts not at all for the rhetorical ubiquity of "cox-ucker."

Maybe it's just a funny word. Say it ten times fast and it loses its vulgarity, its imagery, and becomes a punctuation mark, a pause for thought, like "you see." As in, "I watch Santo cross the street, you see, and a Chevy come . . ."

As college kids, most of my buddies and I worked jobs during the summers. When we got back to school, our friends would ask us what we'd done for work.

"So wudja do, Ray?"

"Got a job in New Hampshire, Mt. Washington, Cog Railway. Laying track and stuff."

"Tough work?"

"Bet your ass."

Here I'd light a cigarette and figure out how to crank this one up. "Yeah, more work than most people know. Like soaking the cogs."

"How's that?"

"You don't just take a cog and expect it to fit. You've got to mold it first. Shape the way it lies. In the old days, when they first built the road, they had steam ovens for the cogs. Same as when you're sheathing a boat in oak, you put the oak boards in a steam oven until they're soft, pliable, before you nail them to the hull. But up on the mountain, you can't lug around no steam oven, so you just haul a big cauldron up the rails, fill it with water, light a fire under it, and drop the cogs in for about 20 minutes until they're malleable. Me, I soaked the cogs." I'd take another hit off the cigarette.

"Yes," I'd say. "I was a cog-soaker."

I had a friend from Pennsylvania got a job in a mine, had to separate the anthracite from the bituminous, the coal from the coke. His chore was to gather the bituminous and collect it in a burlap bag.

"Me," he said, "I was a coke-sacker."

Another kid, job at a winery, socked corks. Yes, we had a rich variety of gainful employments those summers, us cogsoakers, cokesackers and corksockers.

And, cocksucker, we'd laugh like a bastard.

The official name of the Portugee Club is the Portuguese Independent Band. Don't ask. Nobody knows.

Manny ordered us lunch.

And I used to think Irish cuisine was bad.

It was all on one plate: a side of chicken (as in "side of beef"), potatoes, chourizo (a vile Mediterranean pork-based thing heavy with pepper and hooves and ears), and a mound of giant lima beans cut into little slices like the leftovers of a bris; imagine cross-cut sections of octopus arms (or legs or whatever they are, cocksuckers), only instead of its being a loathsome fish it's a loathsome legume.

The door opened and a blast of cold came in, along with a man with white whiskers. Manny waved him over, bought him a glass of red wine. "Louie, this is my friend Ray. Ray, this is Louie. He's got cancer."

"Sorry to hear that," I said.

"Me too. All over." Which you could take any way you wanted.

Tony, the other bartender, came over and topped off my gin. Manny introduced us. "Tony works on the Big Dig."

The Big Dig is the biggest boondoggle in the history of Boston, maybe in the history of the world. For the past ten years it's made driving through Boston your own personal Viet Nam. There is noise and anger and fear, casualties are everywhere, and there's no exit strategy. There's no telling, day to day, which exit goes where, if anywhere at all, and there are either no signs to help you or there are 23 signs to confuse you. I was on the Expressway last week going to Soundtrack, a studio I've been to hundreds of times. Got off at the E. Berkeley Street exit, heading toward Park Square. The signs pointed to 93N, 93S, Chinatown, Cape Cod, the Mass. Pike, South Boston, New York, and E. Berkeley Street.

I ended up in Charlestown on Route 93N heading toward New Hampshire, with nowhere to get off. Six miles up the road I made an illegal U-turn and sped up the ramp back onto 93S, where the traffic was stalled all the way back to the city.

For this privilege, the citizens of Boston have paid something like 15 billion dollars.

But, as Mayor Menino says, "It's creating jobs."

Tony's was one of them. He drove a rig.

"I swore I'd never drive a truck again. My friend Pete, he went over."

"He did what?"

"He was dropping a load of sand, and went over. Truck got in a rut, like pulling a crab, started leaning left over the guardrail, Pete couldn't stop it. Dropped about forty feet, went up like a flare. DOA at Boston City."

Long pause. We raised our glasses to Pete.

"So why are you driving again, after that?"

"Need the work. I get off at two, here at 3:30. Go home around eight. For this," he spread his arms, indicating the entire barroom, "for this I get a dollar a day, cocksucker."

"A dollar a day?"

"The Club's nonprofit. Does some good for the community. Going to put in Ping-Pong tables down the basement for the kids. I do what I can." He held up the gin bottle and raised his eyebrows at me.

"No thanks," I said.

Louie looked at his watch. So did I.

It was a gold chronometer, a stopwatch as well as a watch, with three dials on the face and two buttons on the side to start-stop and reset the timer. I recognized it from a million years ago when I got my first one.

I asked Louie if I could hold it, look at it for a minute.

"How come you want to hold my wristwatch?" he said. So I told him.

"I'm a copywriter," I said. "I write ads." Brief enough for a tombstone. Here Lies Ray. He Wrote Ads.

"So, you time how long it takes you? For time sheets?"

"No, for commercials. Radio commercials are usually one minute, television spots 30 seconds. Exactly. There's no such thing as a 31-second TV spot, unless you want it to end with 'call 254-13 . . .'"

"So you time the commercials with a stopwatch?"

"Yeah. It used to be a badge of honor. You own a stopwatch, you've earned your stripes. You're a writer. When I wrote my first TV spots I used to call the phone company, there was a time and temperature service, free. Recorded message would say, 'The time is 4:42 and 20 seconds; temperature, 56 degrees. The time is 4:42 and 30 seconds; temperature, 56 degrees.' That's how I timed my first commercials."

I shook my head no to Tony's gin bottle.

"So I went to Hudson Hock, a pawnshop in Park Square, where you could get pretty good value on stereos and guitars and watches and stuff, and I asked if they had any chronometers. The kid said yeah, we got a gold one, and he unlocked the display case. Took out a watch that's the same as yours. 50 bucks."

"But this is a new watch," said Louie.

"Same face design, same brand. Patek Philippe."

"No shit."

"The kid said Jim Britt."

"What kid?"

"The kid in the pawnshop. He said the watch was hocked by Jim Britt."

"Why's that ring a bell?"

"Voice of the Red Sox, early sixties. Before Kurt Gowdy, Ken Coleman, those guys. Great baseball guy, radio guy. They say he was an alcoholic, died a pauper. Jim Britt."

50 bucks. Meaning Britt might have got 25. For his gold shield, his badge, his symbol of having arrived.

I used to have this fantasy: I'd be walking home from work one night and someone would ask me, "Spare change?" And I'd look down in the gutter and there would be Jim Britt, cold and dirty and hungry. And I'd say to him, "Mr. Britt, I'm a fan of yours. You were real good at what you did. And I'll not only give you some money, but I'll make you a deal. You clean up your act, dry out, I'll help you get back into radio. And I'll give you this."

With that, I'd show him the watch, the talis-man. And tears would come to his eyes, along with resolve. "Who are you?" he would say.

"I'm Ray Welch.

I'm a copywriter."

I gave Louie back his watch. He looked at it funny. We said goodbye.

"Thank you," I said to Tony. "Oregano."

You ever come to Bristol, you stop by the Portugee Club, okay? Order the special and ask for a dry Beefeater martini straight up. But before you get there, pick up a sandwich, to go, from Santoro's, and bring your own bottle.

Art Direction / Tom Simons and Anthony Henriques

the cutting room floor

When they hear you're writing a book, people you've otherwise found to be sensible citizens lose all sense of reality and suddenly become experts on books. Especially on what should go into them.

You will be amazed at what you'll learn. For example: things that should go into the book needn't have anything to do with what the book is about. It is enough that the things be interesting on their own hook. At least to the person telling you that you ought to put it in The Book.

Your stories from childhood are interesting on their own hook, over the years taking on mythic qualities that nobody picked up on at the time.

All these tales deserve inclusion.

Once when I was a kid I got bit by a skunk. The circumstances were a little strange in that in order to get bit by a skunk I had to have been hunting with a guy named Duke, with air rifles and a can of beer I'd lifted from the family refrigerator, and Jack Babson would have had to come running, out of breath, shouting, "Fellows, there's a skunk trapped in a cellar and we must rescue him!"

the cutting room floor

Now, almost fifty years later, I see this as a non sequitor. That there was a skunk stuck in a cellar did not inexorably require its being rescued. Let alone by me and Duke and the Babson boy. But at the time there was a certain inevitability to it. One that required The Three Amigos to slither on their bellies across the dirt crawl space of a summer home sub-basement, and to face death in a furnace pit, all the while two of the Amigos thinking they were playing some sort of funny trick on Jack Babson.

Boy, wait till the guys at the gym hear what Duke and I pulled on Jack. How we told him to climb down into this furnace hole, make friends with a skunk, and while you pretend to read your watch, Jack, just scoff up the skunk by the tail, so he couldn't spray one, and scramble back up out of the hole with a rescue. A hell of a plan.

Jack did as he was told. He went down into the pit, befriending beasties of the wild. He grabbed the tail. He wound up and flung the skunk.

the cutting room floor

And all at once Duke and I were staring at the business end of a pissed-off skunk, at point blank range. (No matter what they may have told you in school, it is not an inky black cloud of stench that blasts out of a skunk's backside and makes you vomit. It is colorless.)

I lifted the skunk by the scruff of its neck and tried to throw it back into the hole, where Jack was heaving his guts out. But the beams supporting the house, just above the crawl space, impeded one's pitching motion, and the best I could do was slam the poor animal into the ground. Again and again. All the while trying to slide backward under the timbers and pipes and cobwebs, trying to scramble outside before tomorrow's headlines in *The Gloucester Times* would scream "Local Youths Killed by Skunk Smell under Summer House. Guns, Alcohol Involved."

the cutting room floor

Outside now, I still had the skunk by the neck, which was straining to get the head into biting position.

Skunks are strong.

This was not part of the script. We had no plan.

The skunk did.

Had my hero Mark Twain been present, he might have said, "And therein lies the chief difference between skunk and man." And if he had, I would have kicked him in the nuts.

Skunk incisors are about a foot long. Or at least seemed that size when two of them sliced through my thumbnail and wouldn't let go until Duke whacked the creature unconscious with the stock of an air rifle and we managed to pry the jaws apart.

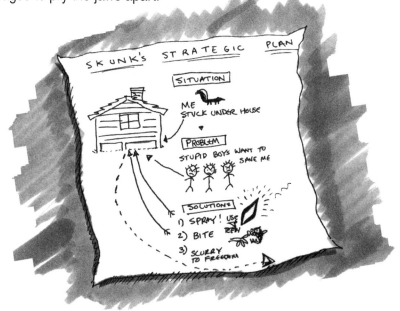

the cutting room floor

Now, on one level, this is an interesting story. On another, it has no place in a volume called Copywriter, whose scope extends not much further than the field of advertising and stuff that happened to me while I was a part of it. The title is not *Copywriter: The Early Years.*

My friend Tom Mauro says "Well, it's a poor book that excludes interesting stories." And then he says, "Take the one about when my father's boss showed up at the house dressed like a marshmallow." Stories about Marshmallow Man, and stories about skunks, they have no place in a book like this.

But we're not talking just about stories here. We're talking as well about people who suddenly remember they have an artistic streak that's been kept under a bushel too long. And so do their relatives.

the cutting room floor

"My cousin Pete takes pictures for Rhode Island Farms and Wetlands. He took a picture of Bristol from a helicopter. Let me give Pete a call. What are you paying these days for aerial shots?"

When I phoned Geoff Currier and said I needed a picture of his long-dead Labrador hound, J. Mary Currier, he told me, "Sure, Joyce took a wonderful shot of her and me sprawled out like we're sleeping. Alongside each other. I'll send it to you."

What I got in the mail was a heavy package padded with crumpled newspapers. To keep the glass from breaking during transit. The glass in the frame of the snapshot of the dog. The photo was not only framed, meaning, when you go to scan it, you can choose to have the picture in focus or the frame in focus, but not both. It was in color. The dog was one amorphous blob of Hershey-bar brown with no distinguishable features. (As if you or I can tell one Lab from another anyway.) And the picture is stuck to the glass.

You can't even steam it off.

The Cutting Room Floor

So here I am at my kitchen table with a knife in one hand, and in the other, this unprintable framed photo of a dog. There is nothing you can do with garbage like this.

Then there are my multi-talented cronies at Aidan's Pub. Poets, musicians, artists . . . collaborators to a man.

I was sitting at the bar with John Whistler, ragging on the meal I'd recently been tricked into eating at the Portuguee Club, a dish whose main ingredient I alleged was "snout."

"That could be a nice illustration for the book," said John.

"The hell you talking about."

"A line drawing of a snout."

"Line drawing of a snout you say."

"Yes." He took out his pen and ripped a piece of newsprint from The Providence Journal and drew a pig's nose. "There," he said. "A snout."

"Jesus, John, can I have this for my book?"

"Will you pay me for it?"

"Sure. How much?"

"A dollar."

"I'll give you a nickel."

the cutting room floor

John thought it over. "That would make me a professional artist, right? And when people ask me what I do for a living I could tell them I do lots of things. I'm a financial counselor, I'm an artist . . ."

"A published artist, John. Don't forget published."

I shouldn't have said that.

Because the joke was getting dangerously out of hand. Whistler was beginning to think I'd actually use his wretched rendering. In my book.

"Hey, everyone," he said, buying a round for the bar, "Ray's going to use my drawing in his book!"

How am I going to tell him "No, no, Johnny, that was only a joke; I can't really put that in the book"?

Well, Whistler is a big boy now, and he'll just have to suck it up, won't he.

Art direction / Brian Heil and Dan Reeves
Illustrations / Dan Reeves

Appendix

"Geoff Currier and J. Mary" photograph by Joyce Currier

"Snout: Portuguese Haute Cuisine" by John Whistler